This wonderfully complex, smart, sweet, sexy woman who was wearing his ring. On her engagement finger.

Jonas had to keep the fake part of this exercise in the forefront. But hadn't it moved out of that territory last night? Hadn't he just been thinking they could take it beyond the weekend reunion—after he'd won the bet—and see where it went?

He was never confused! He was not going to let confusion rule now, not this late in his life.

He was keeping his eyes on the prize! But his eyes moved to Krissy.

His hand in hers was a mistake. He loved touching her, casually like this, as if it was the most natural thing in the world.

Come to that, it feels like the most natural thing in the world.

Matchmaker and the Manhattan Millionaire

—

Cara Colter

Recycling programs
for this product may
not exist in your area.

ISBN-13: 978-1-335-56690-4

Matchmaker and the Manhattan Millionaire

Copyright © 2021 by Cara Colter

All rights reserved. No part of this book may be used or reproduced in
any manner whatsoever without written permission except in the case of
brief quotations embodied in critical articles and reviews.

This is a work of fiction. Names, characters, places and incidents
are either the product of the author's imagination or are used fictitiously.
Any resemblance to actual persons, living or dead, businesses,
companies, events or locales is entirely coincidental.

This edition published by arrangement with Harlequin Books S.A.

For questions and comments about the quality of this book,
please contact us at CustomerService@Harlequin.com.

Harlequin Enterprises ULC
22 Adelaide St. West, 40th Floor
Toronto, Ontario M5H 4E3, Canada
www.Harlequin.com

Printed in U.S.A.

Cara Colter shares her life in beautiful British Columbia, Canada, with her husband, nine horses and one small Pomeranian with a large attitude. She loves to hear from readers, and you can learn more about her and contact her through Facebook.

Books by Cara Colter

Harlequin Romance

A Fairytale Summer!

Cinderella's New York Fling

Cinderellas in the Palace

His Convenient Royal Bride
One Night with Her Brooding Bodyguard

A Crown by Christmas

Cinderella's Prince Under the Mistletoe

The Vineyards of Calanetti

Soldier, Hero...Husband?

Housekeeper Under the Mistletoe
The Wedding Planner's Big Day
Swept into the Tycoon's World
Snowbound with the Single Dad
Tempted by the Single Dad

Visit the Author Profile page
at Harlequin.com for more titles.

Praise for
Cara Colter

CHAPTER ONE

THIS WAS WHY, thought Krissy Clark, she had been avoiding Match Made in Heaven. It felt as if there was a possibility her aunt Jane could walk into the cluttered, tiny Queens office at any second. Krissy looked down at the file on the desk in front of her. It had been left open, as if her aunt expected to get right back to it. No doubt she *had* expected to get right back to it.

Make the first call, Krissy ordered herself.

She looked down at the file. It had a picture of a man stapled to an application form. He was on the better side of sixty, bald and bespectacled. His timid smile was so darn hopeful. All she wanted was a name and a phone number, but instead her eyes grazed the first heading.

What do you do for fun? Nothing naughty, please.

Krissy snapped the file closed. She did not want to know what—she looked at the name in bold, black Sharpie on the front—what Alexandro Helinski did for fun. This was why she could not take over her aunt's business. She didn't have the people skills. The instincts. That almost magical intuition Aunt Jane had possessed.

It had been three weeks since her sixty-six-year-old aunt had died, killed instantly, struck by a car, just down the street from here.

Things had to be dealt with, and yet Krissy couldn't even make a decision about what to do with the ashes.

Spread them in the place I love most. That was what Aunt Jane's will had said. But all that came to Krissy was Macy's!

On a more practical level, the clients needed to be called just in case they had missed the obituary. There might be refunds owed. The office needed to be cleared, or another month's rent would come out of the small bank account Krissy found herself in charge of.

Her aunt had done it for love. If the bank account was any indication, there was no money in the matchmaking business.

And there it was. The real reason Krissy could not take over this business—aside from the fact she was deliriously happy with her own life—was simple.

She did not believe in love. Or at least not the happily-ever-after variety her aunt sold.

Come to think of it, Krissy had not really believed in much that Aunt Jane had believed in: horoscopes, cards, premonitions, reincarnation, life after death. Aunt Jane had claimed she still spoke regularly to Uncle Elias, who had died the year before Krissy was born, which was twenty-three years ago.

And yet, despite not sharing a belief system, she had loved her aunt madly: admired her ability to be genuinely herself in the world, even when that self was a little left of crazy. Compared to the rest of her family, Jane seemed downright sane.

Krissy looked at the flashing red lights on the answering machine. Forty-two messages? She, herself, was not sure she got forty-two messages in a year. Still, listening to the messages might be a better place to start than with the files. She had managed to procrastinate so long it was now too late in the evening to be phoning people, anyway.

Her hand hovered over the play button, then dropped away. She rested her chin on it.

"Auntie," she said out loud, "if you can hear me, I need a sign."

Of what? That her aunt was, somehow, okay. That death, as her aunt had always believed, was just a transition, not an ending. That the aunt Krissy had always counted on to make her feel safe and loved in the world was still there, in some way, supporting her and guiding her.

Krissy immediately felt ridiculous. She was a university graduate. Her major had been in science. She loved systems—unlike the one she had grown up in—that had rules and predictable outcomes. Now she was in her second year of teaching. It was kindergarten, a daily hotbed of chaos and emotion, and yet she was proud of how she used her pragmatic nature to be the port of calm in that sea of tiny challenges.

She was an expert at detaching from emotion and all its foibles. It made her an excellent teacher; it had allowed her to build a perfect life. A few months ago she had bought her own tiny house, and now she had added a dog to the picture she was building.

Okay, the dog, a rescue, was maybe not quite as imagined, but—

Rap. Rap. Rap.

Krissy let out a little squeak of surprise at the firm sound and then laughed at herself, and at how hard her heart was beating.

For a moment, had she really believed her beloved aunt was knocking?

"No," she said out loud.

Yes, a voice inside her whispered.

The sound came again, more insistent. Not from heaven, after all, but from the direction of the front door. She squinted in that direction. It was dark out, nearly 10:00 p.m. A shiver ran up and down her spine, and not because a wind, too chilly for the first week in June, chose that moment to rattle the door.

There was a man standing out there, his knee-length black coat unbuttoned to reveal long legs in knife-pressed dark slacks, an expensive belt, a tailored shirt, a bold tie. He had dark leather gloves that he was slapping with faint impatience against his wrist, as if he expected her to jump up and open the door, despite the Closed sign, despite the fact it was an unusual hour, despite the fact she was in here alone.

Krissy regarded him for a moment. She did not go for blond men. Actually, there was quite a long list of the kind of man she did not go for, which explained why she was single.

And blissfully so.

Still, she could almost hear Aunt Jane's voice.

"Darling, I know I could make you the perfect match if you would just give me the chance."

And Jane was nothing if not tenacious. Just before she had died, she had called, breathless with excitement.

"I found him. I found the one for you."

There is no *one* for me, Krissy had told her aunt, not for the first time. Her aunt, of all people, should understand Krissy's allergy to relationships.

But the fact that Krissy had decided against entanglements of the permanent variety didn't mean she didn't enjoy the odd outing, a date, a *peek*. If Krissy was watching a movie, or studying cologne ads on the train, her ideal man was not blond. He was the quintessential tall, dark and handsome.

The man at the door was tall, and he was handsome. He was broad at the shoulder, narrow at his hips, long in his legs. His face was *GQ* gorgeous—a wide, intelligent brow; high cheekbones; dark whisker-shadowed jaw; perfect nose; firm lips.

Under the outside light, his eyes appeared midnight black. The dark whiskers and eyebrows, the dark eyes, made the blond hair a bit of a shock. In fact, he radiated successful—very successful—businessman, but his hair was wheat and platinum, something sun-kissed and surfer-off-the-waves about it that was in sharp and intriguing contrast to the rest of his image.

He cocked his head at her, and Krissy gave herself a mental shake. She pointed at the Closed sign that hung in the door, and then at her watch.

Charades: too late to be calling on a closed business. She pretended to dismiss him, by looking down at Alexandro Helinski's file. She opened it officiously, being careful not to look at that question.

What do you do for fun?

That man outside the door looked like he might know a thing or two about having fun... Not that she cared!

The second question on Match Made in Heaven's application form.

What would you describe as your life philosophy?

Alexandro had answered, in a firm hand,

Take the high road.

Something sighed within Krissy.
Rap. Rap. Rap.
She deliberately looked at the next question, instead of looking up.

What do you consider the most important attribute in another human being?

Alexandro had answered Honor.

Krissy thought *this* was a man she would be
interested in meeting. If he wasn't sixty-eight!

Her visitor at the door was not getting the
message. He rapped at the door again. She
glanced up, irritated. She was not opening
the door to a complete stranger. It was practically the middle of the night.

When he saw he had her attention, he held
something against the door, a small white
card. His business card? Why would she open
the door for a business card? Any ax mur-
derer could have a card printed!

Still, from the look on his face, he wasn't
going anywhere, one of those extraordinarily
good-looking men far too used to getting his
own way. Making it very evident that she was
annoyed, Krissy got up from the desk and
stomped over to the door.

She looked at the card being held to the
glass.

It wasn't a business card, after all. It was
an appointment card, for Match Made in
Heaven, the blanks filled out in her aunt's
own distinctive handwriting.

Jonas Boyden had an appointment here.

And the date on it was for today. At 10:00
p.m. What was her aunt thinking, conduct-
ing business at that time of night in this quiet
Queens street?

Now what? Krissy couldn't even make
phone calls to tell people her aunt had died.
It felt even worse to try and shout that horrible announcement through the thick glass
of the doorway.

Besides, one of her aunt's many strengths
had been her tremendous ability to vet people
before they ever got through the door. Jane
had taken to the internet like the proverbial
duck to water. She was proud of announcing
that she could find out anything about anyone.
She had loved playing online detective. Krissy
sometimes felt Jane enjoyed rejecting clients
as much as she had enjoyed accepting them.

Jane claimed her high reject ratio made
people want her services even more, had made
them feel special to be chosen by her, part of
an elite group. Having now seen Match Made
in Heaven's bank numbers, Krissy wondered
if Jane might have carried that philosophy a
touch too far.

*I always had everything I needed. Open
the door.*

Now she was going to talk to the dead?
Obviously Krissy should not have come here

tonight, even if it had felt pressing. It was too soon. The wound was too fresh. Krissy was not her normal self.

"Can we speak for a moment?"

His voice was muffled by the door. Even so, it had a sensual rasp to it. He gave her a small smile, no doubt contrived to make him look harmless, but the smile, revealing beautiful, even, brilliantly white teeth, made him more dangerous than ever.

Not in the stranger-danger way, but in the way that showed he had extreme confidence in his own ability to charm, and no doubt that confidence was well earned.

Jonas Boyden was exactly the kind of man who was extremely dangerous to a woman who was deliriously satisfied with her choice of a solitary existence.

What he definitely was not? Alexandro Helinski. He was not the kind of man who would have needed the kind of services her aunt offered. Ever. He was the kind of man women flung themselves at, and he carried himself with that aggravating self-assurance of a man accustomed to that.

So who was he? A lawyer? Someone here about bills? A business associate of her aunt's? Why at this time of night? But if he wasn't a client, that might mean that he had not been vetted thoroughly. Still, that was her aunt's handwriting on the card.

Krissy wished she had the nerve to tell him to come back tomorrow, but wasn't that what she was doing with all her aunt's affairs? Trying to put them off until tomorrow? It would just take a few seconds to find out what he wanted, break the bad news to him and send him on his way. It might even be just the impetus she needed to get started on all the things that had to be dealt with.

She clicked the dead bolt and pushed the door open a miserly crack.

An alarm began to shriek. It was loud enough to wake the dead, which given her aunt's current status—and her request to hear from her—was terrifying.

The sound paralyzed Krissy, her feet felt pinned to the floor by it. She wanted to just cover her ears and shrink away from the appalling noise. Instead, she jumped away from the door and scanned the wall. Sure enough, there was a keypad, flashing the message *Enter Code Now.*

Code? She didn't have a code. She had come through the back door. She hadn't even been aware there was an alarm system.

"May I?" Without waiting for her answer, the man opened the door fully and stepped through it. A blast of wind came through with him and lifted some papers off her aunt's desk and tossed them onto the floor. Really, it was like meeting the hero in a gothic novel!

He closed the door quickly against the wind, barely spared her a glance, but even so she noted his eyes were dark: not black at all, but a rather astonishing shade of blue— navy, like the deepest part of the ocean.

His presence, the broadness of his shoulders under that exquisite jacket, made the cramped office seem even smaller. Between an over- flowing bookshelf and a file cabinet with open drawers, it felt as if there was no place to go.

She squeezed back against the wall as he studied the control panel. Even so, his shoul- der brushed hers, and a lovely scent wafted off him. It transported Krissy. The wailing of the alarm took a back seat. It was as if the solid strength, the timelessness, of a pine for- est had come through the door with him.

He was that kind of man who made a woman, even one as deliriously independent as her, feel that if they did rely on someone other than themselves every now and then, it wouldn't be a weakness.

It would be utterly delicious.

CHAPTER TWO

JONAS FELT AS though his eardrums were being ripped out of his head. The woman, obviously wary of strangers, as she should be, was gazing at the control panel with consternation.

Madame Cosmos—his secret name for Jane Clark—was nowhere to be seen. Was this the woman that she had come up with for him?

She was definitely not his type. Not a speck of makeup, almost owllike with those huge dark eyes behind large glasses. Masses of luxurious dark hair were pulled into a sloppy bun. She was not very tall and she was not exactly plump, but gave the impression of hiding generous curves under an unflattering outfit.

Then again, given the task he had given Madame Cosmos, *not his type* might be exactly what was called for.

But yoga pants and a mustard-colored, too-large sweater? Sneakers? No one met their match like that. Plus, it was more than evident she had been surprised by his arrival.

No, she was obviously an office assistant, working late, or maybe she was even the cleaning staff. Madame Cosmos had obviously forgotten him. Was that so surprising, given what had appeared to him to be flakiness at their initial interview? She had asked him, with grave interest, his zodiac sign.

"What's the code?" he called over the din.

The woman covered her ears and glared at him. It was really no time to notice her ears were tiny and sported prim little pearls. Her withering look indicated it was more than obvious she did not have the code. Her eyes sparkled with warning not to mistake her for an idiot.

He could step back into the night and let her deal with it. But he had important business with her boss—*satisfaction guaranteed, indeed*—that could not wait. It was June already. The long weekend in July was looming large.

He stepped up to the box and lifted the panel on it. No code, and surprise, surprise, no off button. Beside the alarm panel was the electrical box for the office. It might be a better bet. He opened it, found the main power switch.

He glanced at her, and she nodded. He flicked the switch.

They were plunged into instant darkness, but the silence was blessed.

He took a step back and gazed at her in the faint glow of a streetlight coming in the window. He could see the rich shine of her thick chestnut hair, piled up carelessly on top of her head.

He had a shocking sense of wanting to slip those glasses from her face, a shocking desire to know what her hair would feel like beneath his fingers if he freed it to cascade around her shoulders.

Where had that thought come from? Jonas frowned. He was not a man given to that kind of wayward thought, nor was she the kind of woman who inspired them.

In fact, her look leaned toward a comfy Saturday-at-home-with-the-cat.

Still, there was a certain voluptuousness to her, a plumpness to a full bottom lip, a spark in those eyes that hinted at passion for a man patient enough to coax it to the surface.

What she wasn't, was any kind of a—

"Bimbo," Madame Cosmos had told him with a sigh, after having just met him, scanning him with shrewd eyes that had felt as if they stripped him to his soul. *"You have a*

long history of dating exactly the wrong kind of woman."

Despite the fact Jane had come so highly recommended, Jonas should have cut and run right then. It was a measure of his desperation—or maybe his obsession with winning—that he had not.

What the young woman in front of him wasn't, Jonas reminded himself sternly in an effort to stay on track, was Jane Clark. In fact, she was the antithesis of the highly recommended matchmaker who had the flair and panache of a carnival fortune-teller.

He had a sudden, exceedingly uncomfortable thought. What if he was meeting his match? Right now? What if this was who Madame Cosmos had picked for him? Not just the antithesis of herself, but the antithesis of the kind of women he normally dated?

It seemed like the kind of stunt the old gal might pull. *Just throw them together, surprise them with each other and see what happens. See if they sink, or see if they swim.*

It made him look at the woman in front of him in a different light. An exceedingly uncomfortable one. She was definitely not the kind he had ever gone for. Something bookish and girl-next-door about her.

"I have an appointment," he said, "with Madame...er... I mean, Mrs. Clark."

"Canceled," she said abruptly. "You'll be called." She nodded toward the door, dismissing him.

Jonas absorbed the shock of being addressed like that, but had to admit he was reluctantly intrigued. There was that spunkiness again, that warning not to mistake her for an idiot.

Jonas took a deep breath. *Let's find out*, he told himself. "I'm Jonas Boyden."

"I saw that on the card. What's your business with Jane?"

"I'm a client."

He braced himself for her to arrive at the same realization he just had, to say, shocked, *But I am, too.*

Instead, she said, "A matchmaking client?" She looked very skeptical.

"Indeed."

"You are not."

There it was again. A feistiness that belied the more muted bookworm look. She was actually calling him a liar, which should have been insulting. Instead, he was intrigued.

Jonas cocked his head at her. "Excuse me?"

"You're no Alexandro Helinski."

"Who?"

"Never mind. What would a man like you need a woman like my aunt for?"

Her aunt. Not his match, then. He was instantly relieved. And maybe, ever so slightly, disappointed.

"A man like me?"

"Don't women flounder at your feet?"

"Maybe I don't need that kind of woman." *Bimbos.* "The floundering kind. I hired your aunt to find me a match."

"What kind of a match?" she asked, reluctantly curious, suddenly round-eyed, behind her glasses.

"A match made in heaven," he said dryly.

"You were going to let my aunt pick a wife for *you*?"

"Isn't that what she does?"

Krissy felt she probably looked like a fish gasping for air. She snapped her mouth, gaping open with astonishment, closed. A man like this would be using her aunt's services? There was no sense being curious. Her aunt's services were no longer available.

But curious she was. "You can't find your own wife?"

"I'm not exactly looking for a wife."

Of course he wasn't!

"The circumstances are unusual," he continued. "Your aunt wouldn't normally take my kind of request, but I needed a partner—temporarily—and she took pity on me."

A temporary partner? He was darned right that was the kind of request Jane would not have entertained! But she obviously had, though it was hard to imagine anyone taking pity on this self-possessed man.

"I need a fiancée," he said, "and I just don't have the time to sort through profiles, to research backgrounds, to assess suitability, to gauge compatibility. Your aunt promised to do all those things for me. She guaranteed satisfaction."

"A temporary fiancée." It sounded perfectly appalling. What had auntie been thinking?

"It's complicated. I won't bore you with the details."

Krissy was pretty sure she wouldn't be bored.

"But I do need to see your aunt. Urgently."

"I'm sorry, Mr. Boyden, my aunt won't be helping you." Krissy struggled to tell him that her aunt had died, but somehow saying the words made it seem all too real all over again. She took a deep breath, needing to get the words out without crying. Why couldn't he just leave, as she had asked him, and she could call him when she was more composed?

His brow lowered as Krissy's silence lengthened. Mr. Boyden was not used to people not helping him!

"I have a contract," he said. "Not to mention having made a small fortune of a down payment."

"Can you just leave me a business card?" Krissy said, suddenly weary. She was not going to be vulnerable in front of this man, announce to him bluntly her aunt was now deceased. "I'll call you next week and we'll arrange a refund."

"Next week?" he said dangerously. "Next week is too late. I don't need a refund. I need to be engaged!"

"That's ridiculous. And impossible."

"She hasn't done it, has she? She hasn't made me a match."

"No, I don't believe she has. I can't—"

He regarded her stormily for long enough that it felt as if she was going to stop breathing.

"What about you?"

"Excuse me?"

He stepped toward her. He didn't reach out and he didn't touch her, and yet Krissy felt as if he had taken her glasses off and was planning on running his hands through her hair.

"Yes, you'll do," he decided, a touch too

clinically. "There's a little of that librarian look to you. Wholesome. The girl next door. Yes, you'll do."

Krissy's heart was beating madly, as if he *had* removed her glasses.

"I am not going to be your temporary toy!" she said. She wanted to sound firm, but her voice had an unfortunate squeak to it. *Librarian, indeed.*

He cocked his head charmingly at her, as if he was not being completely ludicrous.

"Toy," he said, his tone mulling. "No, no, I don't think so."

Why on earth would she feel vaguely insulted by his dismissal?

"That could lead to complications," he explained gravely. "That's in part why I turned to your aunt. No complications. Still, we would need to get to know each other first, before we made it official. It's important to know each other."

"You think?" she asked. He seemed to miss her sarcasm.

"It's for a family reunion in the Catskills, the long weekend in July. My sister would know instantly if you didn't know what my favorite color was. Restaurant. Movie. That kind of thing."

What kind of weakness was it that Krissy

suddenly wanted to know what his favorite color was? Restaurant? Movie? Plus, the long weekend in July. She had always spent it with Aunt Jane, who knew, as her own parents had not, that occasions—birthdays, Christmas, Easter, the Fourth of July—were important to families.

His invitation felt like a reprieve from the looming weekend alone, but more, it felt as if she was being invited to step into the pages of a story, a very interesting story with all kinds of twists and turns and characters she knew nothing about.

Krissy did not like temptations. She did not appreciate her sudden awareness that the nice, safe, predictable life she had so carefully constructed for herself might be slightly… Well, boring.

That was her aunt's word, after Krissy had brushed off her enthusiasm about having found the perfect man for her.

You're too young to be so set in your ways, so allergic to adventure. Life is not meant to be such a bore, my dear.

"Come on," he said persuasively. "It will be fun."

Fun. So no matter what he said, there was an element of her being his toy in there. Temporarily.

What do you do for fun?

Krissy considered what she would put on that application form. She walked her dog. She planned lessons for her class. She took in the odd Broadway show. She read.

She resented Jonas Boyden for holding out this to her, like a carrot in front of a donkey reluctant to take even one step. And she detested herself for *wanting* something.

But what?

Something just a tiny bit unexpected in her routines, she admitted slowly. For life to surprise her.

As if it hadn't done quite enough of that! And what she needed to remember from her past, from growing up caught between a battling mother and father, was that the surprises were rarely ever of the pleasant variety, and that there were few things in life more dangerous than hoping it would be better. Her aunt's sudden death was a case in point about the nastiness of surprises.

"No," she said firmly.

He frowned, just like the kind of brooding hero who blew in on a dark night, just like the kind of man who rarely heard the word *no* from anyone, let alone a member of the opposite sex, just like a man who could turn a woman's world upside down without half trying.

He considered her thoughtfully, then lifted an elegant shoulder. "All right," he said, giving up with surprising ease, as if suddenly having a fiancée, or a toy, or whatever, didn't matter to him a whit.

Was she annoyed by that? No, she told herself firmly. She was relieved. That was all.

CHAPTER THREE

KRISSY'S RELIEF AT having the issue of being Jonas's temporary toy settled was short-lived. Over the broadness of his shoulder, she watched a police car slide silently up to the curb. Two officers got out, settled their hats on their heads and turned narrowed eyes toward her aunt's office.

"Oh, no! They must be responding to the alarm. I'd better go tell them that—"

Jonas stayed her with a hand on her shoulder, then turned and looked over his own shoulder. "I don't think you want to go racing out there when they could well think a robbery is in progress."

His hand on her shoulder did not feel in any way domineering. His voice was deep, quiet and reassuring. She felt protected. Again, Krissy allowed herself a sense of it being okay, every now and then, to rely on someone else. As long as it didn't become a habit!

When his hand slid away from her shoulder, she realized how easily leaning on someone else could become a habit. Even an addiction!

The policemen were eyeing the building warily. It occurred to Krissy that she and Jonas were just two shadowy figures standing in a darkened building that an alarm—that had not been turned off properly—had gone off in.

"What should we do?" she whispered uneasily.

"Just wait. Let them come to us. Don't make any fast moves once they come through that door."

She gulped and scanned Jonas's face. He looked perfectly calm. In fact, irritatingly, he looked as if he might actually be delighting in this.

He glanced at her, his smile seeming to confirm he might be enjoying this just a tiny bit too much—a man who embraced the kind of adventures she was utterly allergic to!

"You can prove you should be here, right? On your aunt's premises?"

Her mouth opened. Then closed. He was obviously trying to rattle her. On the other hand it was a *burglar* alarm. It seemed there was a fairly good chance that she and Jonas were going to be presumed to be burglars!

"What kind of proof would they want?" she asked him, trying not to let on she felt quite nervous.

"I don't know. A note from your aunt? Evidence that you work here? Don't worry, though. They'll get it all sorted out. Probably at the station."

A flashlight shone through the window, bouncing off her aunt's cluttered bookshelves and file cabinet, but it just missed catching Krissy and Jonas in its beam.

"The police station? Am I going to get arrested?" she squeaked.

"It seems doubtful, but not impossible. If you do—"

"Yes?"

He leaned toward her and smiled a rather wickedly satisfied smile. "I can give you a get-out-of-jail-for-free card."

She scanned his face. She knew he was kidding, and was not kidding at the same time. He oozed the confidence of that kind of man, the kind with the money and the connections and the innate sophistication that made people respect him and bend over backward to solve his difficulties.

"Why in the Monopoly game of life do I always end up in jail?" she wondered out loud. "Instead of owning the hotel chain?"

Jonas threw back his head and laughed when she said that. His laughter was like that get-out-of-jail-for-free card he had just offered. It seemed almost enough to erase the predicament they were in.

Unfortunately, both policemen froze outside, alerted by the sound that someone was in the building. They looked so *ready* to handle whatever jumped out at them. Krissy had a new appreciation for the difficulties of the job they were doing.

"Okay," she said, "I'll take that get-out-of-jail-for-free card."

"Well, nothing is actually *free*," he said easily, his tone playful, as if he hadn't even noticed guns. "We'd have to negotiate terms."

She could not help but appreciate how his lightness was distracting her from the very real intensity of what was going on—policemen advancing toward them assuming there were criminals in the building.

"If I go to jail, I'm sure you'll be going to jail, too!"

He showed her the appointment card in his hand. "No, I don't think so. This appointment card will show I had legitimate business here."

"Well, then, you can vouch for me."

"Or I could say I interrupted a burglary in

progress, depending how willing you are to negotiate terms."

Jonas was teasing her. He was doing it on purpose, proving that Krissy was not hiding her nervousness as well as she might have hoped. The policemen had moved out of her range of vision.

"It's not funny," she told him. "What are they doing out there?"

"Calling the SWAT team."

She gasped.

"I was kidding. I think they are looking for signs of a break-in. Broken glass. A kicked in door. If you do go to jail—

"You don't really have a get-out-of-jail-for-free card," she said irritably. He obviously did not get the seriousness of this situation.

"No, but I have the next best thing. A team of lawyers on call. I'll lend them to you."

She groaned.

"For that cost we have yet to negotiate," he said silkily.

"What kind of man has a team of lawyers on call?"

"One who handles a lot of real estate."

"You ended up with the chain of hotels!"

"Very true."

She refused to be impressed. "That isn't the right kind of lawyer!"

"It would probably do in a pinch."

"What's the cost?" she asked Jonas. He was so calm and so confident that it eased a bit of her panic. He was actually *playing.* Unfortunately, he was just the kind of man you would want in your corner if you were about to be arrested.

And, she warned herself, that you could get addicted to playing with!

"Fiancée for a weekend."

The door flew open. The flashlight blinded her.

"It's a false alarm," Krissy cried. "I have a right to be here! I'm the owner's niece."

She glanced at Jonas. He didn't look terrified at all, but faintly amused, as if this was going to be a great story to tell at the office. She was pretty sure he winked at her.

To be honest, if you had to find yourself in a situation like this, somehow it was a man like this one you would want at your side.

How could she possibly know *that*?

Jonas shot his companion in crime a look, but she obviously was not seeing the humor in any of this, especially now.

"We just have to ask a few questions and then we'll be on our way," one of the policemen said.

"Perfectly understandable," Jonas replied.

She shot him a look that said she was relying on him to get her out of this, to be her prince, riding in on a white charger to save her. He hadn't had anybody look at him like that since his mother and father had died.

And then his sister had cast him as her hero. According to her, he had lived up to her expectations.

But he had paid a price for shouldering all that responsibility very young. Ever since then, he'd avoided having people rely on him. According to his sister, Theresa, who liked to offer her opinion even when it hadn't been asked for—especially when it hadn't been asked for—it was her fault he had become the quintessential bachelor, so allergic to commitment he couldn't even have a houseplant in his apartment.

And now Theresa and his brother-in-law, Mike, were gleefully getting ready to cash in on a bet he'd made a long time ago, when he was young—and possibly full of tequila.

Be committed by thirty or—

"You obviously don't look like our typical burglars, but due to the circumstances if you could tell us your business here at this time of night, it would be appreciated."

"I have an appointment with Jane Clark," Jonas said.

"See, that's the problem," the policeman said. "She died last week, and there are actually people scummy enough to read the obituaries and target her premises."

Jonas felt a shiver of shock go through his system. He glanced at the woman, and could see she was fighting back tears.

"He's not a scumbag," the quavering voice beside him offered.

Given that he had held her over a barrel with his offer to help her for a price—even though he had been kidding—Jonas thought that was very generous.

"It's my fault. I should have been phoning people and letting them know about Aunt Jane. Just in case they hadn't done what, apparently, scumbags do and read the obituaries. I'm supposed to be looking after things."

She was so genuine that both the policeman relaxed noticeably. "Your aunt was a much-loved fixture in this community," one of them offered. "She'll be missed by all of us."

She hiccuped. And then a tiny little noise escaped her, like the mew of a hurt kitten.

All three men in the room reacted in the same way—silence, stiffening body postures, an exchange of panicky looks.

A crime in progress was one thing. Largely manageable, a defined response called for and given, an event with a high possibility of a defined and satisfactory ending.

Tears falling—female tears—was quite another.

Within minutes the explanations had been given and accepted, the men in blue had reset the alarm and left with what appeared to Jonas to be uncommon haste.

He could see why. With those huge dark eyes misted with tears, and that full bottom lip trembling with emotion, she had become the kind of woman any man feared most.

Totally vulnerable. Soft. Needy. One who could use a strong shoulder to cry on. He could, unfortunately, picture her clinging like a limpet, sobbing against him, him patting her back…

Stop it, Jonas ordered himself. He slid a longing look at the door that the other men had just exited, took a deep breath and decided to finish this business as quickly as possible.

"Your aunt died?" Jonas said. "Why didn't you say something instead of letting me act like a complete jerk?"

"Maybe not a complete jerk," she said with

a little sniffle. "Fifty percent. You did offer me a get-out-of-jail-for-free card."

"Only not for free," he reminded her. "Why didn't you tell me? Right away?"

"I couldn't bring myself to shout it through the door. I've been having trouble letting people know. I think it helps me keep the reality of it from setting in. I know lots of people thought she was eccentric—

Madame Cosmos, he thought guiltily.

"But she was the most loving person I ever knew. She was the only person in my family I could count on. She was—"

And then she was crying. Big sobs that shook her whole body, exactly the kind of sobs he and the policemen had been trying to head off at the pass since the clouds of that particular storm had first gathered in her eyes.

"I thought I could just send you a letter. And the refund, so that th-this didn't happen."

What was a man to do? Jonas looked longingly at the door one more time.

"Hey," he said, trying for his most empathetic tone, "it's okay."

"It's not okay!" she cried. "I loved her. I loved her more than anyone in the whole world!"

Empathetic tones were probably not his

strong suit. Her distress required a response from him, whether he wanted to give one or not.

Like a man going to the gallows—a man with not one single option left—he went to her.

"It's going to be okay," he said softly. The reassurance had not worked the first time, and it did not work now. The tears were streaming down her face. It was a good thing she didn't have on any mascara! A wail of pure despair came from her.

With no options left, he folded his arms around her.

His last hope was that she would be sensible—she looked like the sensible type—and that she would push him away.

But she did not. And oddly, he did not feel as if he had just climbed the stairs to the gallows. As she nestled into him, a lovely warmth enveloped him. He could feel her tears puddling on his shirt, and after hesitating for just a second, his hand found her hair and he stroked the wild, springy silk of it.

"I'm so sorry," he whispered over and over, his tone as soothing as he knew how to make it. Touching her hair seemed to be releasing a scent that reminded him of the bouquet of fresh spring flowers he had given his sister for Mother's Day. The aroma was fresh and light and ever so faintly spicy.

"Th-thank y-you." She didn't attempt to pull away. "I'm not usually so emotional."

"Ah."

"Really."

The really was followed by a hiccup. Adorable.

He acted fast. "I withdraw the proposal. The fiancée for a weekend, the whole fake mate thing."

She gave him a watery smile at the *fake mate* reference, then tilted her head and looked up at him, gauging something. Apparently, she reached the wrong conclusion, that he was a decent guy.

"These might be the dumbest words I ever said," she said softly, "but why don't you tell me why you have a sudden, urgent need for an engagement? My aunt must have thought your reasons were compelling. I might consider your offer, after all."

Now that he had actually felt her soft curves pressed against him, now that his shirt was wet from her tears, now that the enchanting scent of her hair was burned into his brain, probably forever, now that he had found her hiccup adorable, that didn't seem like it was a very good idea.

He stepped back from her rapidly and looked at her, took in those huge eyes, tears studded in the lashes and strands of luscious hair just beginning to pull free from the clasp that held them, the plump lip, that looked freshly licked, somehow, quivering.

Jonas was pretty sure he needed someone *not complicated* and he was pretty sure this woman in front of him would not fit that criteria. At all.

Her name, provided to the police, came to his lips. "Kristen—"

"Krissy," she corrected him.

"Krissy, it's okay. I'll figure out something else."

"But now I'm curious."

He suddenly did not want her to be curious about any part of his life. It felt extremely dangerous. There was an expression: curiosity killed the cat.

Only in this circumstance, the cat could be him!

CHAPTER FOUR

"I'M VERY SORRY about your aunt," Jonas said with formality, backing away from Krissy slowly, like a man backing away from extreme danger. He felt the door behind him. He put his hand on it. *Have a nice life*, he wished her silently.

"Wait! They reset the alarm! We will have to go out the back."

There was no *we*. Or at least after he escaped out that back door there would be no *we*.

"Look, I'm going to leave, too," she said, her composure returning and her tone soothing, as if she was talking to a flighty animal that was about to bolt. "We can go together. If it's not too much trouble, perhaps you could walk with me? I have to get to Penn Station to get my train home. You could fill me in on the details as to why you need a fiancée."

"Uh—"

"Fake mate," she said with way too much enjoyment. "You don't mind, do you?"

Actually, he did mind. He suddenly didn't want her knowing any of the details of his quest for a temporary arrangement of the fiancée kind. On the other hand, he did not want her going out the back door by herself, or walking by herself, either. And Penn Station at this time of night?

"Where's home?" he asked reluctantly.

"Sunshine Cove. It's a little hamlet in the Hudson Valley—

"I know where it is." A memory tickled. "Is Moo-Moo's still there?"

She smiled. Now there was a dangerous thing, far more dangerous than the tears that still wetted the front of his shirt. That smile—along with the fresh memory of her hair, wild and springy under his touch—confirmed his thought that lurking under that deliberately frumpy librarian look was something else entirely.

"Still there," she said. "The best strawberry milkshake in the world."

Jonas formed an unfortunate picture of those lush lips closing over a straw.

"A strawberry shake?" he scoffed, partly to erase the visual. "You don't waste a trip to

Moo-Moo's and have a strawberry shake. You have the Triple Chocolate Volcano Sundae."

She frowned at him. "You needn't say that like a strawberry shake is boring."

"Well…"

"They use real strawberries!"

This, right here, was why he needed to cut his losses. She was prepared to defend a strawberry milkshake, as if he had somehow called *her* boring, and not the milkshake. And for some reason, instead of cutting his losses, he was prepared to goad her on.

"Caramel Cream Banana Bliss, Gooey Gluey Fudge Cake, Thunder Mountain Raspberry Dazzle or, wait for it, Strawberry Shake."

"Yes," she said stubbornly.

"Every time?"

"Sometimes I have a vanilla cone," she said, as if this was an act of defiance that she was prepared to defend to the death.

"Now you're just trying to bug me."

She was silent.

"I suppose they use real vanilla?" Jonas asked.

"They do. You can see the pieces of ground bean in the ice cream."

"Well, that's exciting."

"We all have different ideas of what's exciting."

That made him look right at her hair. And then her lips. And then, hastily, away. He stuffed his hands in his pockets and rocked back on his heels.

He wondered, a renegade thought that he completely failed to head off at the pass, if they weren't talking about ice cream, what she would find exciting.

"You're very familiar with the menu," she said, her tone a little stiff, as if he had managed to hurt her feelings. Which he probably had. He wasn't good with the sensitive type of woman. She had claimed she usually wasn't emotional, but he was seeing no sign of that.

"I did try to work my way through the entire menu," Jonas admitted proudly. "Back in the day, Moo-Moo's was a big outing for my family."

It was the kind of memory that he, allergic to sensitivity, avoided. Still, it pushed in, the four of them piling into a station wagon for a rare day away from the failing family resort. The day would be laughter filled, love filled. That thing called family, feeling so steady, so safe, so strong, despite the cloud of financial insecurity they had lived under. How wrong a man—a boy at the time—could be in his sense that things could last forever.

Still, Sunshine Cove was exactly the kind

of place he would picture Krissy living: one of those satellite enclaves served by commuter trains, the quintessential Hudson Valley town with mature trees and old manor houses tucked back on big grassy lots, and a sleepy main street that felt like a homecoming.

"I think I had better—" *cut his losses* came to mind. And yet that was not the direction he was moving in. He knew what he was going to do. Felt weirdly as if he *had* to do.

Jonas heard a sound. What was it? A heating system with a squealing belt turning on? A cat fighting in the alley? For some reason, it shivered along his spine. "Did you hear that?"

"No, what?"

"It sounded almost like the alarm going off again, only way more quiet."

Krissy tilted her head at him.

Jonas could not tell her the full truth. It sounded like someone in the distance laughing. He was not sure he had ever heard Madame Cosmos laugh, but he was pretty sure if she did it would have the alarm-like stridency of a cackle of pure delight.

It made him reconsider what he was just about to offer to do. After all, what was the point of Krissy thinking he was the kind of perfect gentleman a strawberry shake woman like her would require him to be? And what was the point of leaving himself open to her curiosity when he had decided Krissy as his fake mate would be way too complicated?

"I don't hear anything," she said decidedly after a moment. "You think you had better what?"

What, indeed? he asked himself.

"I think I had better drive you home," Jonas said.

Krissy could hear the reluctance in his voice. Well, who could blame him? It was a long drive, and the round trip would take him deep into the night. Plus, she had cried all over him, and he had decided, on the basis of milkshake choice, that she was boring.

She suspected his motive was pity. Who wanted to be pitied by such an excruciatingly attractive man?

Still, it was so tempting! A car instead of the train, an opportunity to bring some of these boxes home. Plus, it would be so quick. And her dog had now been home alone for way too long.

Crusher. Was she actually dreading going home to the new resident?

Of course not! In fact, for the dog's sake alone, she should accept the ride. But underneath all those very good reasons to accept Jonas's offer, Krissy was aware of something else. Despite the disagreement over what was exciting in ice cream products—or maybe because of it—she *wanted* to spend more time with him. She was intrigued. She wanted to unravel the mystery of why Jonas, a man brimming with such confidence, such a sense of himself, was searching for a fiancée.

All the more reason to say no, as if a pro and con sheet was being built in her head. Despite his association with her aunt, he was a complete stranger.

On the other hand, she always said no. It was her default answer for nearly everything, including trying other items on the menu at Moo-Moo's. Why not say yes for once? Why not be open to life being surprising?

It occurred to her that maybe she just didn't want to be alone.

"That would be very kind," she shocked them both by saying.

Moments later, weighed down with boxes, they emerged from the alley behind Match Made in Heaven. Jonas led her down the street and stopped at a sleek-looking car that was not like anything she had ever seen before.

"What is this?" she asked, annoyed that

her voice had a reverent whisper to it. Obviously, the kind of car a man like him—a Triple Chocolate Volcano Sundae guy—drove. Or a James Bond type. Or a business tycoon.

Her own car suddenly seemed as boring as her ice cream choices, an economical subcompact that was good on gas and was a less than exciting shade of white. In fact, her car was about the same shade as a vanilla cone.

This car was vintage, very sporty and low-slung. Without knowing a single thing about cars, Krissy knew it was powerful. It glinted a deep and glossy muted pewter under the streetlight.

"It's the cause of all my problems," Jonas said with rough affection. He opened the passenger-side door and leaned in, stowing the box he was carrying in the back. She ordered herself not to look at the way his jacket rode up and his slacks stretched tight, but part of her mutinied against the order.

Jonas was a beautifully made man!

She was blushing by the time he turned back to her, but thankfully it was dark enough out that he seemed not to notice. He held open the door for her, and she slid into the seat. She was immediately embraced by the scent of rich leather, mingled with another scent that she recognized from when he had held her. Tangy. Clean. Male. The end result was one of being immersed in the man's subtle sensuality.

A moment later he got in the driver's side, turned the ignition and the car growled to life.

"It's a Jaguar," he said.

He pronounced it *Jag-guare*, which for some reason was nearly as swoonworthy as him leaning over to stow those boxes.

"Nineteen sixty-four," he said proudly.

"And how is it the cause of all your problems?" Krissy ventured, after he had pulled smoothly into traffic. She had to admire the way he drove, handling the powerful car with the casual inborn confidence one might associate with riding high-strung horses.

"It was the first major purchase I ever made. Way back in the day. It was kind of like my *I have arrived* statement. I love this car madly."

She slid him a look. In the glow of the dashboard panel, it was evident all of that was true. He had definitely arrived. And he was in love with his car. She wondered how many women were jealous of his passion for the car, and Krissy vowed not to be one of them.

"And how is it the source of all your problems?"

"I acquired it the same week my best friend, Mike, asked my sister, Theresa, to marry him. We started our business together. That's how he celebrated his arrival. I bought a car. He proposed marriage."

Jonas's voice was rough with wry affection as he continued. "I thought they were both way too young to be making that kind of commitment. I told him I, personally, would be waiting until I was thirty. He scoffed at that, not seeing me as the commitment type, ever.

"Somehow, way too many celebratory shots of tequila later, I was betting the car—this car—that I would be as committed as he was by the time I reached the age of thirty. That is a date that is rapidly approaching and that my now brother-in-law is gleefully ticking off on his calendar."

"That's silly. He won't hold you to it."

"Oh, he will, and with delight, I might add."

"It's not like it's a legally binding contract, for heaven's sake."

"I shook hands on it. That's binding to me."

What do you consider the most important attribute in another human being?

She remembered how she had loved Alexandro's answer. Honor.

"That's a very twisted kind of honor," Krissy decided, for both Jonas's benefit and her own. "You're willing to *pretend* you have made a commitment to win a bet you shook hands on while clearly inebriated."

"Exactly," he said, and glanced over at her. He grinned with utterly enchanting mischievousness. "I guess you have to take into account the basic competitiveness of my relationship with Mike. If he won this bet, he would lord his ownership of this car over me for the rest of my life."

"That is a long time to have something lorded over you," she admitted. She felt like she was learning quite a bit about Jonas. He was fun loving. This *problem*—how to keep his car—was a game to him.

It was all quite charming. But buried in there was a larger message, the reason for the bet in the first place, the reason it had become a problem at all. The man was commitment phobic.

It would be best to accept this ride home from him and call it a day. Tangling with him in any way—particularly in a phony engagement way, fraught with the potential for complication and emotional catastrophe—

was inviting peril into a life she had made deliberately safe.

Too safe, she chided herself. Strawberry milkshake safe.

"Are you close to your family?" she asked.

There was a long pause. She glanced over at him. She could see a sudden tension in his shoulders and around his mouth.

"What's left of them," he said quietly. "My parents were killed in a car accident when my sister and I were in our late teens. I think it made Theresa and me closer. And now that family includes Mike. And two monster nephews."

His voice was ragged with both pain and affection.

In the muted light of the dashboard, Krissy saw the utter torment of a man who had loved completely—and lost—cross his handsome features. It was far from the playboy image that she generally would associate with commitment phobia, and somehow it made him so much more compelling.

"I'm so sorry," she whispered.

"It was a long time ago," he said brusquely. "I'm not sure why it came up at all. I guess thinking about the excursions to the ice cream parlor brought it to mind."

In a moment of madness, egged on by the

purr of the car engine and deep leather seats, heady scents, and most of all, by his unexpected vulnerability, Krissy took a deep breath.

Her aunt had always told her life could be an adventure, and here she was. Despite all her efforts to avoid it, the unexpected had found her. This morning the closest Krissy had come to excitement for a long, long time was stepping in dog doo.

But now, she was in a gorgeous car with an even more gorgeous man, and life for the first time in a long, long time seemed like it held the potential for... What? Almost anything.

"I'll do it!" she blurted out before she could change her mind.

She tilted her head to look at him, waiting for him to smile. Or laugh. She thought the twinkle would return to those deep sea blue eyes, and that he'd turn to her with gratitude and say something cool and approving like, *Thatta girl, say yes to the adventure.*

Instead, humiliation flared to life and then deepened as the silence stretched out between them, and he looked straight ahead. There was a faint frown around his mouth.

Jonas obviously had decided she wasn't suitable!

Krissy debated, briefly, leaping from the moving car. It was barely moving, because they had just stopped at a traffic light. But she couldn't even order a Triple Chocolate Volcano Sundae, let alone jump from a car to save her wounded pride.

Besides, there was no point letting him know how wounded her vanity was. And on a practical side there were the boxes stowed in the back to think about. She couldn't just abandon Aunt Jane's things over a point of pride.

So instead of making the dramatic escape she longed for, Krissy sank back in her seat and followed his example by looking straight ahead. She tried not to gasp when he changed lanes, and the car shot forward as he passed a truck.

See? The hard beating of her heart told her the sad truth. It was too late. She had gotten herself into a strawberry milkshake kind of rut, and you couldn't just decide to get out of it. You couldn't change who you basically were—and nor should you want to on the basis of how damnably attractive a man was.

She just wasn't a take chances kind of person.

CHAPTER FIVE

JONAS SLID KRISSY a look. She had her hands folded primly on her lap, and was looking straight ahead. Still, exactly because of her schooled lack of expression, he knew how deeply he had hurt her feelings.

Which was precisely why she would not work as a fake mate!

He couldn't have a woman whose feelings were easily hurt. Or a woman who made him blurt out his secrets, either. Why had he told her about his parents? He rarely mentioned the family tragedy to anyone. His pain was intense, and it was *private*.

But it also made him the man who most understood the desolation of loss, and he wanted her to know she was not alone with all those feelings. Jonas also found he could not be the kind of man to be responsible for hurting her more deeply than she already was. He had to break the silence that was causing her so much pain.

"I think you're just too close to your aunt's death," Jonas said carefully. "Obviously, it's too much to ask of you right now."

"All right, I understand," she said, clearly unconvinced of his sincerity, clearly determined to take his rejection of her as fake mate personally and as an insult.

"Good," he said, knowing he could only make this worse if he kept trying to convince her.

Then she said quietly, "Though I have to say, the last hour has been the most respite I've had from that awful swarm of feelings since I got the news my aunt had died. Her death feels like a nightmare I just don't wake up from."

Jonas remembered oh, so well the intensity of that awful swarm of feelings, that sense of having entered into a nightmare that wouldn't go away.

Don't do it, he ordered himself. But human decency required more of him. He'd known she was the kind of woman who would require more from him.

"Well, if you think it might be a distraction from your grief..." His voice drifted away.

"I was trying to do you a favor," Krissy

said, her voice low, faintly wounded, but faintly angry, too. "Not have you take pity on me and feel like you're doing me the favor. Besides, I think based on my milkshake choices, you have found me lacking in some way, so I withdraw my offer."

He slid her another look. She turned her head quickly to look out the window, as if something really interesting was happening out there, when in fact they had just left New York and were now flying along in near total blackness.

How had this happened? He now felt like he should be *begging* her to do what he least wanted her to do, which was accept his original poorly conceived proposition.

"I haven't found you lacking," he said.

"Oh, please." She did not turn to look at him.

"No, really. It's not that at all."

"Uh-huh."

"Krissy, to be honest you just seem like the kind of woman things could get really complicated with."

"So, it wasn't all about giving me room to grieve!" she said, triumphant at having caught him in the little white lie. Told for her own good, but no brownie points there.

And thinking of her own good, Krissy was

a little too smart for it. And definitely too smart for *his* own good, as well.

"In what way am I complicated?" she said dangerously.

In this way, right here, he thought, but wisely refrained from saying it. There would be no way to answer that question correctly, so he said nothing.

"Like I might not understand it was a game? Like I might forget it was all fake? Like my grief might make me needy and clingy? Like I might find you irresistible and cross the line? Like I'm just some pathetic homely girl who would be so far out of her league—"

"Stop it! You are neither pathetic nor homely. This is exactly the problem—you're complicated."

"And you like uncomplicated." She said it as a statement, not a question.

"Yes," he said, relieved that she got it. "That's what I asked your aunt for. Uncomplicated. Someone who would understand the clearly defined parameters of our arrangement from the beginning."

"I can't believe my aunt went for that."

"Well, she did. Not only did she go for it, but she took a big deposit and she guaranteed my satisfaction."

"Well, I offered to fulfill the contract, and you said no, so—"

"I didn't exactly say no."

"Your unenthused silence spoke volumes."

"I was thinking!"

"Yes, about how to get out of your ridiculous offer and my misguided acceptance of that offer. Which I accepted to help you. But you thought it would be too complicated, so now you have gotten out of it. Your contract with my aunt is null and void. And I'm not giving you a refund, either!"

"That's fine," he said tightly. "No refund is required."

What was required was that this awful journey with her be over. He was not cut out for rescuing damsels in distress. He was not a man accustomed to second-guessing himself, but he wished he had not offered her a ride home.

He was so glad when they pulled up into the tiny hamlet of Sunshine Cove. He put the address she gave him into the GPS he'd added to the car and avoided its instructions to take Main Street, which would bring them right past Moo-Moo's. Instead, he took the alternate route.

He pulled up in front of a cottage. Once it must have been the carriage house for the manor house that shared the lot. Now, its postage-stamp-size yard had been separated from the larger house with its sweeping lawns, by a thick hedge of lilacs, heavy with wilted blooms. The carriage house itself was tiny and looked like something out of a fairy tale—paned windows and pansy-filled window boxes, Tudor timbers exposed under the curving A of the roofline.

Krissy scrambled out of the car as if she was trying to escape something that smelled bad. He would have been quite happy to roar away, but unfortunately he had to help her with her boxes.

"Just put them there," she ordered outside her front door, not looking at him, fishing for her key. The scent of finished lilacs was heavy in the air.

A dog that sounded huge howled on the other side of the door. He decided he might be wise to make his exit before the beast was unleashed.

"Well," he said with relief, "it's been nice meeting you. Again, I'm sorry about your aunt."

"Likewise," she said. "Sorry for your losses. Nice meeting you. Have a nice life."

That was supposed to have been his line! Before he could make good his escape, she said, "And just for your information, I would have been the safest bet ever for a fake mate, because I am *never* getting married. Ever. There was absolutely no possibility of a phony engagement to me becoming complicated."

Jonas highly doubted that. It was already complicated, because he wanted to ask her what had made her so vehement on the topic. Instead, he turned quickly and went back to his car.

Escape was within reach. Once he got to that car, he never had to see her again. Fake mate, indeed. Not complicated? From their very short acquaintance it was more than evident to him that Krissy was too sensitive, too smart and way too sensual in that understated way of hers.

Even glancing back at her, seeing her standing under the glow of her porch light, he had a renegade thought what it might be like if he had delivered her home after a date, what it would be like to be standing there debating whether or not to kiss her good-night.

You couldn't have thoughts like that with a fake mate!

He was sliding into his car when she got her key in the door.

The dog that erupted out that door was

every bit as big as it had sounded like it would be: a monster of a dog, a creature of near-mythical proportions, its gray head the color and size of a rotted pumpkin.

It leaped at her with joyous enthusiasm that might have been adorable in a Pomeranian but was frightening in such a large dog. Its immense paws found her shoulders, and a huge tongue lolled out. Partly laughing, and partly outmatched, she turned her face away, but the dog was not to be deprived of its kisses.

She lost her balance in her twisting effort to avoid the worst of the slobbering affection and went to her knees. The dog shoved her the rest of the way over, and she was completely pinned as the giant dog jumped on top of her and swiped at her face with a tongue about the size of a paint roller.

Jonas suddenly understood the lack of makeup and the casual outfit. His escape thwarted, he got back out of the car and strode up the walk. Before he reached them, the dog froze, cocked his head and took off running.

Jonas arrived at Krissy and offered his hand. Her laughter had dried up the second the dog took off, but she still had that "just kissed" flush on her face.

He was so irritated—with himself for being

so aware of her or with her easy acceptance of the dog's unacceptable behavior he wasn't sure—that he might have used a little more force than was absolutely necessary to yank her to feet.

She fell against him, and her hair finally pulled completely free from the clasp that had held it so sloppily in place. It cascaded around her shoulders in a rich wave of color, scent and curl.

For the second time tonight he found the lusciousness of her curves pressed full-length against him. How much could a man take?

Krissy could feel the hard line of Jonas's body and she tilted her chin and looked up into his face. The sudden downturn of his mouth—not happy to be rescuing her *again*—did nothing to detract from how handsome he was. In fact, it brought his every feature into sharp focus: the intensity of his eyes, the height of faintly whisker-shadowed cheekbones, the fullness of his lower lip, the faint cleft in his chin. His eyes trailed to her hair and then to her lips, before they came to rest, darkened, on her own eyes.

She knew he was every bit as aware of her as she was of him. Something unexpected sizzled between them.

She had opened herself up to being surprised by life and here it was.

She wanted to taste him. She wanted to kiss this man who was a virtual stranger. Was this the *complication* he had spotted so readily? Was this the danger?

Of course it was. She looked at the sensuous firm line of his lower lip. She should pull away, and yet she felt herself pull in closer, drawn to him helplessly, like a magnet to steel.

The bark of her dog in the distance jolted her out of her foolishness. She pulled away from Jonas and scanned the direction the dog had gone.

There he was, at the base of a tree, barking at the neighbor's cat that was glaring at him from a low branch.

"Crusher!" she called.

"Crusher?" Jonas said with a groan. "Seriously?"

The dog spared her a glance. The cat took its opportunity and leaped from the tree. The dog bolted after it.

She took off after Crusher, and with a sigh of pure resignation, Jonas took off with her. When the dog and cat went over a fence into a neighbor's backyard, Jonas put one hand on the fence and vaulted over it. She heard the distinct sound of his pants ripping as she scrambled after him.

She was fairly certain, as they dashed through darkened backyards, they were going to have their second encounter of the evening with the police.

Half an hour later, they finally cornered the dog and avoided arrest.

Jonas took off his belt to use as a temporary leash. There was a large tear in his slacks; the zipper had pulled clean away.

She started to laugh.

He glanced down at himself, and then back at her, sheepish.

"You're blushing," she crowed.

"I'm not," he denied firmly.

"And you're wearing tighty-whities!"

"I'm not!" he said.

"Well, what are they then?"

His blush intensified. He glared at her. "You said you wouldn't be complicated, but here we are in the middle of the night discussing my underwear."

But then a grin tickled the edges of his mouth, and then a snort of laughter escaped him. In a second, they were both laughing, doubled over with it, the dog bouncing between them, taking turns leaping on them and swiping their faces with his huge tongue.

At last, Jonas handed her the belt leash and pulled off his jacket, and tied it around his waist. He took the makeshift lead back from her when Crusher nearly yanked her arm off.

"Stop it," he told the dog. Or maybe he was telling her to stop it, because she was still giggling, the moment effervescent with surprising delight.

The dog did stop. He quit pulling and walked quietly at Jonas's side, which was a good thing, because Jonas literally had his hands full. Krissy laughed most of the way home as he tried to keep his dignity while he juggled the dog, his beltless pants and his coat cover-up.

It was as if there had been way too much sadness of late, and the laughter had been waiting. Once uncorked, it wasn't going to be shoved back in.

Finally, they were back at the cottage.

He handed her the leash.

"Thank you," she said.

They stood there in awkward silence for a moment. He looked at her in a way that made her uncharacteristic giddiness dry up and her heart stop.

"I have to go," he growled.

"Yes, you do," she said. Even though it was insanely late, and she had to teach in the morning, she had been thinking of asking him in for a drink.

He hesitated. "I was just thinking, that maybe we could make it work."

"Make what work?"

"You know. Fake mate."

So he didn't want whatever had sprung up between them to end, either. Which made the potential for complications seem extremely high.

And at the moment, Krissy, bathed in moonlight and laughter and dog kisses, found she just didn't care.

CHAPTER SIX

"I THINK MY sister and Mike would find you believable. A girl with a dog."

Oh. It was about Mike. And his sister. And the dog. In a roundabout way, the car. It was about everything except what had just leaped in the air, sizzling, between them.

There was no reason to be insulted by that! It reduced the possibility of complications, didn't it?

"Plus, it's evident to me," Jonas said, "you need some help with the dog. There is nothing funny about such a big dog being so poorly behaved. You could have been badly hurt when he knocked you down. What if you'd smacked your head on the pavers? What if that had been a child he leaped on like that?"

These were, of course, valid points, but Krissy's feeling of being insulted grew.

"Crusher is a rescue," she said defensively.

"I haven't really had him long enough to work on his, er, issues."

"Well, start with the name. Because a dog will always live up to whatever name you give it."

"He came with that name."

"You can change it."

"I thought that was bad luck."

"For boats!"

"What would you suggest? Pansy?"

"Better," he said, deliberately missing her sarcasm.

He moved away from her and over to Pansy-Crusher, who was wriggling in anticipation of attention. Jonas studied the dog, touching that one ear torn off in a long-ago battle and taking in that the face was badly scarred.

Jonas turned back to her. "You know it's a possibility this dog is too much for you, don't you?"

That very thought had been niggling at the back of her mind almost since Crush—Pansy's—arrival. But she *hated* that he saw it.

"I'm prepared to do what it takes," Krissy said firmly.

Jonas studied her, then lifted a shoulder. "I guess we'll see," he said. "It would be a trade. I could show you a few things about handling the dog, and if it looks like we're compatible, you could be my fiancée at the reunion. It happens to coincide with my thirtieth birthday."

Krissy had never been to a family reunion. Neither her mother or father had enjoyed good relations with their extended families. Their family of three had lived on a desert island, but not the idyllic kind. Aunt Jane had been the only respite, the only rescue.

So this casual reference to happy family events made Krissy feel an uneasy sense of longing.

He cocked his head at her. "It's at our family resort in the Catskills. My sister and Mike run it now. It's always a fun time."

That uneasy longing grew in the pit of her stomach.

"Family and fun going together," she said, before she could stop herself. "There's a novel concept."

"Your family wasn't fun?" he asked, as if it was shocking news to him that families weren't fun.

Shut up, she ordered herself. "Just Aunt Jane. The rest of it was pretty much a war zone."

His gaze was deep and stripping, loaded with unwanted sympathy. Krissy tilted her chin proudly at him. "Your family doesn't fight?"

"Of course they fight. My sister is downright mean with a water balloon."

That kind of fight seemed so innocent. Krissy felt a longing she had suppressed push against the lid she had put on top of it.

"I'm not sure about the reunion," she said.

"We'll take it one step at a time," he said, his surprisingly gentle tone making another longing leap up deep inside of her.

"Homework," Jonas said, as if it were all settled, "Find a new name for the dog. I'll drop by Saturday. Early afternoon. One-ish, okay?"

He didn't wait for her answer. "If things go well, we'll take a walk downtown with him for ice cream at Moo-Moo's. Who knows? Maybe you'll order something exciting."

He said that as if there was hope for both her and the dog.

Say no, Krissy ordered herself. If she didn't, Jonas would take over her whole life before she even knew what had happened. She'd be renaming her dog and breathlessly anticipating going for ice cream with him and even thinking about ordering something different. She'd be looking forward to a family reunion, to that tantalizing glimpse of what normal was.

She didn't say no.

Instead, she watched in silence as he turned away from her, stopped at his car door to remove the jacket tied at his waist, then slipped inside and drove away.

"I feel as if I've just survived a hurricane," Krissy confided in Crusher.

And that, she told herself, explained the euphoria. Completely.

A few days later, on Saturday, getting ready for Jonas's arrival, Krissy told herself firmly it was not a date.

So how did she explain the pile of clothes on her bed, tried on, reviewed, discarded? The dog was now nestled in the middle of them.

"Get off the bed, Hans," she said to Crusher, trying out yet another name. The dog did not respond, and she shook her head. "Maybe better for a German shepherd," she decided.

The explanation for the number of clothes discarded was actually quite easy.

"It's like a job interview," Krissy told herself. "If you're going to be a fake mate to a man like Jonas Boyden, you have to look the part."

Of course, it was complicated, just as he

had somehow known all along it would be. Because it was very difficult to find an outfit that was absolutely beguiling while looking like it was not trying to be, and that was also appropriate for a session of dog training.

And added to all that, it had to be appropriate for eating ice cream afterward, the outfit of a girl who was not afraid to be bold in her choices.

Krissy finally settled on a pair of wildly flower-patterned end-at-the-calf leggings and an oversize white T-shirt. She put on a pair of hot pink running shoes that matched one of the flowers in the leggings. She added a chunky, colorful necklace and earrings.

Then she took a curling iron to her hair, hated how it looked—trying way too hard—and scooped it back into a ponytail. Disliking herself for it, she added just a touch of makeup, a bit of mascara, a dusting of blush and hint of lip gloss.

She regarded herself in the mirror and thought she had hit just the right note: spontaneous, sporty, fun, someone not at all concerned about the complications of a fake match.

"What are you doing to me?" she told the urn of her aunt's ashes as she passed the mantel in her small living room.

Jonas arrived promptly, and she peeked out her front window as he came down the walk. The spring sunlight glinted off the wheat gold of his hair. He carried himself with the supreme confidence of a person who would never give a second thought to outfit choice.

And of course, he had that just right, casual in a short-sleeved navy blue button-down shirt, chinos and canvas loafers. The sunglasses gave him a bit of a film star aura.

She was aware, as she opened the door, she felt extremely nervous.

However, all the effort she had put into making a great first impression on their second meeting was for naught, because the dog bounded out the door.

"Louie," she cried, as the dog leaped up and placed its paws on Jonas's substantial shoulders, "stop it."

Neither the dog nor Jonas even glanced at her.

"Off," he said sternly. "Now."

The dog, shocked and confused by this rejection of his enthusiasm, lowered himself to all fours and then gazed at Jonas with some consternation.

"Sit," Jonas commanded.

The dog sat in three stages: his huge hind end swayed, then inched down, hovering, and then, finally, plopped all the way onto the ground.

"Is Louie what you've decided on?"

She frowned. All that work on the perfect look and not even a *Hello, Krissy, how are you? Looking lovely today, I must say.*

"Not really. I'm just trying it."

"Hmm. It sounds like a name for a dog that would trip over his ears, like a basset hound."

"Well, it won't do for him, then." They both looked at the dog's ears, the one in tatters.

The dog looked like it was considering getting up, and Jonas snapped a finger at him. He nestled back down.

Jonas cast her a glance, finally. "What did they tell you about him at the rescue center?"

He was being so all business. She longed for the laughter they had shared the other night. Should she remind him of his ripped pants?

No! She should keep it all business, too. Even the fiancée part, when they got to that? Especially the fiancée part, when they got to that! But how could you pretend to be someone's fiancée with this businesslike attitude?

She thought of her parents. Civil, but distant, would be an improvement in some relationships!

"I didn't exactly get him directly from the

rescue center," she admitted. "One of the other teachers at school had taken him, and it wasn't working out."

He looked exasperated by that. Where was the man who had made her laugh so hard? For both their safety, wasn't this coolness so much better?

"He wasn't working out for someone else, and so you took him?"

"Artie Calhoun, the fifth-grade teacher, brought him to the staff room one Monday morning. His wife had told him not to come home after work if the dog was still with him."

"The dog was being bad enough it was breaking up a marriage. That would compel you to step in, why?"

A question she had asked herself several hundred times!

"Look at that face."

They both looked at the dog. Hans-Louie, the pansy crusher, lolled out his tongue in a silly grin and did that thing with his eyes where he looked up at them with a certain forlorn hope.

"How could you not fall in love with it?" Krissy asked.

Jonas made a low sound partway between a sigh and a groan. She looked at him. True enough, Jonas did not look like he was a falling-in-love kind of guy. In fact, he did not look like a man who would give his heart easily. To anyone. Or anything.

Not that that was any of her business. Not that she wanted to even think about Jonas falling in love!

That would make their arrangement impossibly complex.

"Anyway," Krissy said, "I couldn't resist him, and he's here and I'm committed now."

Jonas winced at the very word and looked at her warily, as if he had discovered she was the superhero of lost causes.

The dog tried again to get his legs under himself.

"No," Jonas said with the authority of a drill sergeant. Crusher plopped back down, ducked his head and looked contrite as he sneaked looks at Jonas's face.

Jonas sighed again. "I didn't think a rescue center would match him with you. Don't look insulted! It's not personal. The dog may have been a fighting dog, which means he has aggression built into him. It's not a good thing for an inexperienced owner."

"He's not aggressive," she said firmly. "If he was a fighting dog, I think he probably washed out of fight class. He just hasn't had enough love."

Jonas actually groaned. "He doesn't need love. He needs discipline. Do you see how I'm greeting him? I'm not feeding his excitement. When you come home, don't even greet him. Don't even look at him."

"Really?" she asked, appalled.

"When you get home, get a leash and take him for a walk. Don't even go in the door until you've done that. Every single time. Because he's got way too much energy and it's a bad idea to reward that by letting him jump all over you. The affection should always be initiated by you, after he's earned it. And it should *never* involve him jumping on you."

Krissy could feel her back going up. He hadn't even noticed her outfit! Was Jonas always so bossy? Of course he was! He had that look of a man quite accustomed to being in authority.

Still, she bit back her irritation. She'd agreed to this trade. And really, she was being offered what she most needed right now. Which was not a fiancée, fake or otherwise. It was a well-behaved dog.

The kind of companion she could walk into her old age with.

"You seem to know quite a bit about dogs," she conceded.

"We bred, raised and trained hunting dogs

when I was growing up. It was our off-season business."

"Oh, dear," she said. It was time to remind him of the other part of their deal. "I don't know how this is going to be a fair trade when you know quite a bit about dogs. I, on the other hand, know nothing about being a fiancée. Your fiancée."

"What's to know?" he said. "I'll put a ring on your finger. We'll gaze at each other adoringly."

A ring? She hadn't even considered that. And the gazing adoringly part seemed very dangerous, indeed.

"I think the family reunion would be too much," Krissy said carefully, "A whole weekend? It just gives too many opportunities to expose the fact we don't know each other."

"But by then, we will."

"We will?"

"Sure. We'll do a few dog training excursions, I'll take you out for dinner a couple of times. We'll know everything there is to know about each other."

That sounded scary!

"Then we'll go to the reunion, we'll cream all the competition in the water fight, eat too many hot dogs, sing by the campfire, show off your ring."

The picture he painted called to a little girl inside her who had craved exactly that kind of family and that kind of gathering. She had seen such things in movies and read about it in books. Kids at school talked about lives that made her aware that her life—her parents' battles followed by periods of crushing silence—was not normal.

Aunt Jane had known how wrong it all was. She had taken Krissy out of that situation as often as possible. Overnight sleepovers at her great little NYC apartment, trips, excursions, outings. And she had always assured Krissy, whenever they were alone together, that the home situation was not her fault. And yet how could it not be?

How could it not be, when Krissy had been the reason—the accidental pregnancy—that had brought her parents together?

"Besides," he continued, oblivious to Krissy embroiling herself in distressing thoughts, "we'll bring the dog. You'd be amazed how a dog becomes the center of attention. My sister won't notice much else."

Krissy was not convinced the reunion could be a good idea. "I think maybe just dinner to introduce me to Mike and Theresa," she said. "Show them the ring. You can claim

I had a previous engagement for the reunion dates."

"Let's just see how it plays out," he said. "Go get that leash and we'll start."

It was all wrong. Everything about this whole encounter was wrong. He was taking charge completely. He was triggering forbidden longings in her. She had thought it would be fun, but she felt tense. It was supposed to be the prelude to their engagement, but it felt businesslike and calculated. She had dressed up for it!

What was troubling her was it felt as if Jonas Boyden was here out of some unfathomable sense of responsibility for her.

He had been 100 percent correct in his assessment of their situation when he had refused her initial offer to be his fake mate.

It could get complicated between them. Fast.

CHAPTER SEVEN

KRISSY WONDERED IF Moo-Moo's was still on the table? It was such a small thing. It already felt way too large. If it was still on the table, she planned to be shocking. She planned to order the most exciting thing on the menu. She seemed to recall, vaguely, there was an item called Earth Orgasm on the menu, a concoction of organic yogurt, nuts and bananas.

That was ridiculous. She was being ridiculous. Embarrassingly so. She didn't even like nuts! And she wasn't all that fond of yogurt, especially in an ice cream shop.

But it was just more evidence you could not keep things uncomplicated with a man like Jonas Boyden. Particularly if you let your mind wander to orgasms in any form. Krissy did not like being ridiculous.

She was already nervous about the family reunion and it was nearly a month away!

So the best thing to do would be to tell him

the deal was off. She needed to put an end to this now. She didn't need him to help her with the dog. There were thousands of books out there. And videos. She could ask him to recommend a few.

She opened her mouth to say it.

"See?" Jonas said quietly. "This is what you want. Do you see how relaxed he is? That's what you reward."

He dropped down on his haunches in front of the dog and took the big mug between both his hands. He massaged with his palms and his thumbs, pressing deep circles into the scarred face of the dog. Crusher-Pansy-Hans-Louie's tongue fell out of his mouth and he closed his eyes. A moan of pure bliss escaped him.

A light seemed to be shining out of both of them, man and beast.

Krissy watched for a moment, utterly entranced.

She sighed. She would just have to put her own best interests on hold for the good of her dog, she told herself as she went and got the leash.

A rare thing had happened to Jonas when Krissy had opened her door.

He'd been caught off balance, and not entirely because of the dog trying to leap at him. He'd been expecting the woman from the other night, the one with the frumpy sweater and shoes and messy hair and makeup-free face. The one who had brought out a surprisingly protective side of him. And not just because of the dog, though it was more than evident she was in over her head with the mutt.

But his protective inclinations had surfaced more because of what she had said about family and fun being a novel concept. About her family being a war zone. He had thought about that over the last few days way more than he should have. Grief was hard enough to deal with. How did you deal with it alone?

It made him so aware of what a gift his family was. Theresa, Mike, the nephews, but also that brood of boisterous aunts and uncles and cousins who always had your back, who always made sure you knew you belonged to something larger than yourself.

It made Jonas, perhaps foolishly, commit to something: showing her how it could be. He wanted her to experience his family reunion, and somehow the motive of having her as his fiancée had become muddied.

But the woman who opened the door had

replaced the librarian-in-need with a woman who didn't look as if she needed his help at all.

Krissy, in the hot pink shoes and those crazy cutoff tights that made her legs looks endless, looked fun and sexy. She had on a touch of makeup: just enough to make her eyes look huge and gorgeous and to make her bottom lip look full and glossy and tempting. Her hair was pulled back in a stern ponytail, but it showed off the bone structure in her face.

And made him want to send it cascading around her shoulders the way it had the other night.

See? Complicated. He, a person who prided himself on his razor-sharp ability to focus, was off-balance.

A man, Jonas reminded himself, focusing on the only safe thing in the vicinity, the dog, should always go with his first instinct!

He took shelter from the bombarding of his senses by hiding behind what he knew about dogs, which was, thankfully, quite a bit.

As soon as she brought the leash out, the dynamic changed. Jonas became instructor, and Krissy became student.

"Let's start by giving him a name." He snapped the leash on the dog's collar.

"Beauregard!"

"Something short would be better. Preferably one syllable. Beau?"

Krissy actually blushed, as if he had asked if he could be her beau!

"How about Chance?" she said. "I'm kind of taking a chance on him."

"And giving him a second chance. From the look of his face, he's had a hard life."

"Perfect, then!" she said, beaming.

Happiness became her. As he watched the light come on in her face, he felt awareness whisper to life within him. Not just of her, but of what a beautiful day it was. Spring in the air, the leaves and grass nearly exploding with shades of green, the scent of blossoms in warm air, the sky bright blue and cloudless. The whole drive here, he had been so focused on his muddled thoughts, he had totally missed that.

Despite the opportunities for potholes and pitfalls, it seemed as if maybe coming to Sunshine Cove this morning wasn't such a bad road to have chosen, after all. He felt something relax within him.

Jonas demonstrated how to walk the dog in front of her cottage, walking away from her.

"Super relaxed," he said. "No tension on the leash. Expecting him to pace himself to you. You stop, he stops. You pick up the pace, he picks up the pace."

When he turned back, there was something faintly guilty in her face, as if she hadn't just been watching the dog! Unless he missed his guess, she'd been checking him out!

"He's always nearly pulled my arm off," Krissy said, just as if she had not been checking him out. "If he sees something, well, you saw it the other night. A squirrel, another dog, someone who looks friendly, he's off. To be honest, it's made me reluctant to walk him." She seemed to realize she was chattering. She stopped abruptly. She looked anywhere but at Jonas.

It added the most interesting little sizzle to his heightened awareness of the day.

Stick to business, Jonas ordered himself. "This is a big dog. He needs to walk twice every single day. Once in the morning and once at night."

"I know. You said I can't even go inside the house after work until he's had his walk. I can't believe how wonderful he is for you!" she said. Her eyes skittered back to him. This time they didn't skitter away.

There was something intoxicating about being admired by a pretty woman on a spring day. They walked through the sleepy, lovely streets of Sunshine Cove. An old man was getting his garden ready, stringing rows. Children shrieked on a trampoline. A small dog raced up to a picket fence and barked hysterically at them.

It felt as if they were a couple, and it felt shockingly good and not just because it suddenly seemed like he had a very real chance of convincing his sister and Mike this was the real deal and keeping his car.

"I can't believe he didn't acknowledge that dog," Krissy said beside him after they had passed the yappy Pom-cross.

"He needs a leader. He wants one." They arrived at the wide arch that led to the park and pathway that ran along the Hudson. Jonas passed the leash to Krissy. "Now you're his leader."

She took the leash gingerly. She stepped out hesitantly. The dog sensed her lack of confidence and pulled eagerly at the leash when a bike went by.

Jonas stepped in and covered her hand with his, and tugged at the leash. "See? Just a slight correction. Bring his attention back to you."

He seemed to have succeeded at bringing her attention back to himself. And his to her. That scent filled his nose: the spring bouquet freshness of her. The softness of where her skin touched his intensified some feeling of being totally alive.

He could have let go and stepped away, but there were two little old ladies in the distance coming toward them. He didn't want Chance jumping at them.

After they had passed, he moved away from Krissy, aware of his reluctance to break contact with her and annoyed with himself because of it.

The dog immediately sensed she was on her own. It yanked on her, and she lurched forward. Jonas fought the impulse to leap in and rescue her. He couldn't be here all the time. He had to focus on his mission, which was to at least make it safe for her to have the dog, to handle it on her own. The way it was behaving now, she could end up with a broken bone.

"Gather yourself, make him sit, try again."

But now she was rattled and trying too hard, and the dog was confused. Jonas stepped in, took the leash—careful not to touch her this time, Chance was obviously picking up on something agitated—and made the dog sit.

Jonas passed the leash back to her. "No, don't go right away. Make him sit. You decide when to go, not him."

"I'm terrible at this," she decided dejectedly.

"Try this," Jonas said. "Act the part. Shoulders back, long, confident stride. Exaggerate it at first. You're a model on the runway."

She cast him a doubtful look.

"No, really. Just give yourself to it. Lots of attitude!"

He could see the moment she decided she would try it. Her shoulders came back. Her chin went up. With the leash firmly in one hand, she set the other on her hip. She stepped out, long strides, placing her feet one in front of the other, as if she was walking a tightrope with deliberation. Her hips swung. She narrowed her eyes and did a stern little purse with her lips.

Jonas had to bite back laughter. He was tempted to tell her the facial expressions were probably not necessary, at least for the dog's sake, but he was enjoying them too much to stop her.

Chance, sensing the difference in Krissy instantly, came to attention and walked well at her side. Jonas watched from behind them, trying to be teacher-to-student analytical, but he was now aware he was definitely checking her out!

Krissy turned her head back to him. *It's working*, she mouthed, as if it was a big secret they needed to keep from the dog. She seemed to realize he was checking her out. She lost her rhythm and Chance catapulted into her.

Jonas leaped forward and caught her before she fell. The moment intensified around him: her softness, her scent, a pink, plump petal falling from a flowering tree.

Her lips looked as plump and as pink as that petal. A command blasted through his brain. *Kiss her.*

He was so shocked by the impulse that he shoved her away.

"Okay, so modeling material I'm not," Krissy said.

"Actually, I think you nearly had it. But you could try something else. Maybe an actress going up to get your Oscar?"

She made a face at him, gathered the leash and concentrated. He watched her face form into haughty lines. Confident and untouchable, she sashayed forward. Then, really getting into the spirit of the thing, she bobbed her head to the right and left, nodding at her imagined fans. It was hilarious. The dog was taking tentative steps with her, glancing at her face with utter confusion. After half a dozen steps, he sat down in protest.

"I'm not really feeling this," she said. "It's phony—it's not me."

In other words, absolutely the wrong choice for fake mate. She wasn't good at pretending. The dog knew it, too.

"That explains the dog being confused," Jonas said. "But sometimes you can at least fake the body language. Try the queen."

Krissy shot him a look, but gamely recomposed herself. She cupped her hand and marched along with the dog, her face solemn, her hand turning languidly in her impression of the royal wave. The dog was now dragging behind her, shooting Jonas aggrieved looks at what he had created.

"Toodle-loo," she told the dog, in a very bad impression of an English accent. "Come along, now."

Jonas had been trying to hold back, but this cracked him up.

She stopped and looked at him. The dog, relieved, plopped down. Jonas stifled his laughter and moved to them. He tried to convince the dog to get back up. Chance pinned his butt to the ground as if it had been crazy glued.

His stifled laughter broke free. It rolled out of him.

Still with the accent, she said, "Are you laughing at your Royal Majesty the Queen?"

"No, Your Highness." Snort, chuckle, snort.

"The Royal Dog?" she asked, aghast.

"I wasn't laughing, Your Highness. Coughing. See?" He demonstrated a cough, but it didn't work. It turned into a fit of laughter that he had no hope of stopping.

And then she was laughing, too, and the dog got all excited and raced around them, binding them up with the leash.

Somehow, they were pressed together again, and instead of feeling all wrong, a pretense that had gone too far, it felt all right.

She gazed up at him, and he looked down at her. The world—even the dog—faded away. So did the laughter.

CHAPTER EIGHT

HE'S GOING TO kiss me, Krissy thought, dazed by Jonas's closeness, his scent, the glory of his hard, muscular frame pressed against the softness of her curves.

She closed her eyes; she leaned into him. She might have even puckered her lips. Anticipation tingled along every nerve ending. Her heart was beating way too fast. And then...

Nothing happened.

It reminded her, exactly, of his hesitation to accept her offer to be his fake mate the other night in his car. It reminded her how quickly she could be hurt by Jonas when she expected one thing and then another happened. Or didn't happen, as the case might be.

Krissy did what she should have done in the first place. She opened her eyes, sandwiched her hands up between them and pushed. It opened the smallest gap, enabling her to reach down to loosen the leash that was holding them together.

Unfortunately, that required much squirming. The dog, held tight by the wound up leash, cocked his head and looked at them with frank adoration but no cooperation. There was more shared laughter, though now it had the faintest edge to it.

Awareness.

By the time she'd extricated them, Krissy was flushing madly: over the shared merriment and thwarted kiss and the rather intimate contact.

She realized this was exactly what the dog sensed in her all along: a certain reluctance to take control, a certain timidity to take on life on life's terms.

She was with an attractive man. He'd almost kissed her, but then pulled back. She was going to refuse to be a shrinking violet about it.

No! Instead, she would show Jonas what he had missed, what he had said no to. She would make him regret pulling away.

With new determination, Krissy sorted the dog. Once he was sitting at her side, she took a deep breath. She snapped the leash to get the dog's attention, she set her feet.

Krissy didn't want to be an actress or a

model. She had never even wanted to be the queen!

This was an opportunity to find her authentic strength in role models she admired.

"I am," she said firmly, "an Olympic medalist going to the podium!"

She strode forward, radiating confidence, strength, victory. She could feel the relief in Chance. He got it instantly, he stepped it up, he aligned perfectly with her.

"What sport?" Jonas asked.

Krissy had never played a sport in her life.

"A woman warrior," she cried. And she reached up with her free hand and grabbed the elastic that held her hair back. She didn't slide it off, she broke it. Her hair fell free, and she gave it a shake.

"That's it!" Jonas said, his voice low and approving. "That's it exactly!"

But she already knew she had found the sweet spot of confidence she had been searching—maybe all of her life—for. Krissy could feel it in the leash, in the dog's attentiveness to her, in Jonas's attentiveness. She could feel the shift in herself, and she reveled in it.

Thinking of the power and the confidence with which Jonas drove his car, she revved into the next gear. She was the shield maiden going into battle. She was Boudicca, she was Joan of Arc. She stepped out, not with fear. Not with anticipation. Not with awareness of all the bad things that waited to befall her.

With glory! With confidence. With excitement for all the victories that awaited her.

The dog got it. Completely And so did Jonas. Completely.

Krissy felt as if she had stepped out of a shadow she was not even aware she had been standing in. She was enjoying playing the part, and it was wonderful to feel a sense of coming into some part of herself.

That was powerful.

And confident.

And amazing.

And dangerous.

She laughed out loud as she immersed herself in the discovery of her own confidence. She was aware of Jonas looking at her, his smile faintly tinged with trepidation. She was not the same woman who had meekly backed away from his rejection of that kiss a few minutes ago.

They came to a section of the trail where dogs were allowed off leash. Which was ironic, because Krissy was wondering exactly what he had unleashed within her when he had guided her to finding her confidence.

"I don't think he's ready for that," Jonas said.

But she suspected maybe Jonas wasn't ready for things to be completely unleashed, either.

Was she?

"There is a dog park just a little farther up the trail."

"Perfect." He was looking at her as if he wasn't thinking about the dog park, at all.

And somehow that was exactly how it felt. As if this startling, beautiful, electrifying day of discovery was absolutely perfect.

They had the fenced dog park entirely to themselves. They played a game that Jonas said would help Chance learn to come when he was called.

Jonas held the leash, and Krissy went and hid in a small grove of trees. Then she called the dog, and Jonas unclipped the leash. Chance barreled toward her hiding place, ecstatic when he found her, wriggling and ducking and lolling his tongue. But he didn't even attempt to jump on her. Then they reversed it, Jonas hiding and Krissy holding the leash. Chance's joy in the game was utterly contagious. Or maybe it was just a joyous kind of day.

But an hour later, they all lay on the grass, panting, tired, happy. Krissy and Jonas lay shoulder to shoulder.

Like the oldest of friends. Or like lovers. Like any of the young couples out enjoying the park today.

"I think the last time I laughed this hard was at last year's family reunion," Jonas said. "There's a big water fight every year. No restrictions on weapons, just as long as they get you wet. My sister, Theresa, had found this gun that shot water balloons. She was an absolute menace. Mike and I ganged up on her to take it away, and then Simon and Garfunkel—that's what I call the monster nephews—plus their two dogs, were in there, and we were all on the ground, and the rest of the family ganged up on us, until we were wallowing in a mud bog. Those kids and dogs were so dirty, the whites of their eyes were shining."

Krissy tilted her head to look at Jonas. He was smiling slightly at the memory, looking up at the sky, the utter blueness of it reflected in the deep blue of his eyes. Chance had his big head resting possessively on the flat plane of Jonas's stomach, a pool of contented drool darkening a patch of the shirt to black. Jonas toyed with the remnants of that torn ear.

She both liked the way he talked about his family with such warmth and affection, and hated the niggling sense of longing it caused in her.

"Or maybe it was at Gar's birthday that I laughed like this. He was turning four. Simon is six. Gar got a cake shaped like Fuzzy Peter—that's a cartoon character, not something obscene—and then he wouldn't let anyone eat it. He was standing guard over that cake, and Simon sneaked in and grabbed a handful from behind, and then I don't exactly know what happened, but the cake fight was on. Thank goodness we were outside."

His laughter was rich and warm at the memory. That feeling of longing in Krissy intensified. What he was describing was like families she had seen in movies and read about in books, but, except for Aunt Jane, it was the very thing she had never had: connection.

She wanted to know more.

"For research purposes," she said, acting as if her interest in him was purely clinical, so she could play the role he'd assigned, "you really call your nephew Garfunkel? What's his real name?"

"I think it might be Daniel," Jonas said, pretending not to know. "The other one may be Henry. No, Harry."

She laughed, and she could tell that was his intent.

"Boring names to be sure," he continued. "I tried to tell Theresa we could have a family contest to name them, but she's a bit of a spoilsport that way. She seemed to think naming kids was a serious business."

"It is!" Krissy said sternly.

"Uh-huh," he teased her, unconvinced. "When's the last time you laughed like today, Krissy?"

She cast about for an answer. She couldn't find one, which she thought was thoroughly pathetic.

"I teach kindergarten," she said. "There's a laugh a day, for sure."

But his gaze on her seemed to be finding a deeper truth. "You said the other night your family wasn't fun. You said a war zone. I'm really sorry."

She did not want his pity! And yet, his gaze on her, steady, did not hold pity. Sympathy perhaps, definitely compassion. Why did she feel suddenly compelled to tell him the truth?

Maybe so his expectations of her at his family reunion wouldn't be too high.

"The only fun in my family was in the word dys*fun*ctional." What had possessed her to say that? Did she think he would laugh? He didn't. The look in his eyes, the one that made her want to confide in him, deepened.

"My mother and father did not like each other. They got married because they had to.

And the reason they had to was me, the un-expected pregnancy. It was a war zone. They divorced, finally, when I was in my teens, but in some ways that made things worse. I was suddenly at the very centre of every single disagreement. It seemed I was the club they liked to hit each other with."

He sat up on his elbow. He looked down at her. He traced the line of her cheek with a gentle finger.

"Oh, Krissy," he said. "Oh, Krissy."

And for some reason, the way he said her name made her glad she had told him, in-stead of sorry.

It was a part of revealing who she really was, the masks coming off. But being totally authentic with another human being created a feeling of intimacy—of trust—that felt even deeper than if they had given in to the temp-tation to kiss. She was not quite sure she was ready for this.

"So there you have it," she said, trying for a breezy tone. "The reason I, personally, will never get married."

She brushed his finger away from her cheek as if it was a bothersome fly. She leaped to her feet. The dog reluctantly lifted its head from Jonas's lap and gazed at her.

"I had my aunt," she said firmly. "It might

not have been the rowdy kind of fun you just described, but she was the one who saved me, and almost everything we did together was pure fun. She unlocked the secrets of New York for me—the Russian Tea Room, Broadway and, of course, Fifth Avenue."

Jonas looked unconvinced, somehow, that adult excursions with her aunt had replaced the joys of a boisterous family.

"Did you ever do kid things? Ride a bike, play in the mud?"

"Oh, uh, occasionally. I should probably get going," she said, flustered, hating it that he seemed to be able to see her deepest longing. "Home. I have things to do."

Jonas sat up lazily, then stood, brushing grass from his slacks. His hair was slightly rumpled, as if he'd had a nap. In such a self-contained man, the mussy hair was adorable.

But then adorable went out the window as he turned his back to her. "Did I get it all?"

She was in bad enough shape without being asked to inspect the seat of his pants. "Yes," she said, her voice a squeak.

"What kind of things do you have to do?" Jonas asked, turning back to her. She was pretty sure he noticed the blush.

He was going to find out the truth! She played it safe. She was boring! But wasn't that part of what today had ended up being about? Revealing truth?

"I'm doing a spring art project with the kids on Monday. It involves some prep."

"What is it?"

"I'm making them into a garden: each of them will be a flower, with a big cutout that they put their face through. They'll sing a song at assembly next week."

He grinned. "I hope there will be a video."

"And I have to get Aunt Jane's affairs sorted out. I've been procrastinating. I have to get back into her office and box things up. I've given notice already, so I have to get out of there."

He nodded. "Okay. I get it."

She thought of his car and the way he dressed. She didn't know, really, anything about him yet. But he looked like he would be at least as busy as she was and probably more so.

"We'll walk back. I just thought ice cream was on the agenda." He said it hopefully, and it was his hopefulness that did her in.

She had revealed so much of her authentic self to him: some strengths, that inner warrior coming out, and some weaknesses, the childhood on a battlefield that didn't include any water balloons.

And he still wanted to spend time with her? Still, he was willing to put his busy life on hold for more time together?

Something sighed within Krissy. A sigh of pure surrender.

"There's always time for ice cream," she decided, and she was rewarded with his smile, a smile that a person could become utterly addicted to—a smile that could make every other activity and responsibility seem dull and uninteresting—before they even knew what had happened.

Jonas wasn't sure why he had insisted on the ice cream. He was already on sensory overload, so aware of Krissy that his nerves were singing with it.

For one insane moment, wrapped up in the dog's leash, pressed into the soft, womanly curves of her, he had found the temptation of her lips nearly irresistible. Somehow— maybe the warning bell in his brain screaming complications—he had managed, but only barely, not to accept the invitation of her lips.

If the dog had wrapped them in his leash after she had declared she was a warrior and let loose her hair, they'd probably be under a shrub somewhere acting like teenagers.

He should have realized, right then, this was a bad idea. That things were not going to go according to his plan.

His plan? Which was what?

Something utterly trivial like pretending to his sister and brother-in-law that Krissy and he were engaged so he could keep his car. That original mission seemed to be wavering like a mirage on a hot desert day.

Now, even the complication of the near kiss was being blurred with an even stronger desire: to see that playful light come on in her, to see her throw back her head and laugh.

Astonishingly, since he considered himself, unapologetically, the most self-centered of people, he realized it was no longer all about *getting* what he wanted—his car, the satisfaction of winning a bet—but about *giving* Krissy something.

A well-behaved dog. A carefree day. Laughter.

Even if buried in that altruism was an ember of danger that could light his whole world on fire.

They walked down the main street of Sunshine Cove. It was the perfect backdrop for a perfect day: lovely little storefronts under colorful awnings, couples and families, old people and singles made their way in and out of antique stores and bookshops and bakeries. It wasn't summer, but there was enough warmth in the air that the day felt summery and light filled.

Jonas realized the fragrance thick in the air from those abundant flower baskets that hung everywhere was so similar to Krissy's.

"He's never this good," she said to Jonas in that whisper he was beginning to recognize as her keeping a secret from Chance.

"He's tired. You want a good dog? Keep him played out."

"I'm just not sure I have the time."

"Invest three dollars in a Frisbee. That will do the trick."

They arrived at Moo-Moo's. It was under a pink-and-white-striped awning, white painted wrought-iron tables and spindly chairs on the sidewalk patio outside the front door. Jonas realized he had not been here in years, not even with his nephews. It occurred to him he avoided the places where the memories were the sharpest, and that this was one of them.

"I'll stay outside with the dog if you want to go in and order," he said, realizing this had been a mistake. He did not want to go in there. He reached for his wallet.

"I'll get it," she said.

"No, this is my deal." A reminder to them

both, hopefully, that this was, in the end, a business arrangement, an understanding between two people.

She looked as if she planned to argue, but then, as he passed her some money, didn't.

"What would you like?"

"Surprise me," he said, realizing handling that small challenge might reveal even more of the secret side of Krissy to him.

Chance flopped down under the table, settling on his feet.

"Hey, buddy, you're cutting off circulation," he told the dog, who ignored him.

Jonas watched Krissy through the window. Studying the menu, looking at the display cases. It was silly, but he couldn't wait to see what she chose.

A few moments later she came out of the ice cream store, laden with a tray. He was not sure why he was so disappointed. It was a small thing. Krissy had decided not to surprise him, at all.

CHAPTER NINE

On the tray Krissy was balancing was her strawberry shake, served in the old-fashioned way that made Moo-Moo's such a sought-after summer destination. The shake came in a tall thick frosted glass, and extra milkshake that couldn't be fitted into the glass came in the steel mixing container with it.

Jonas saw that for him, she had chosen the Triple Chocolate Volcano Sundae.

And, of course, she had a treat for Chance.

Still, watching her come toward him with that tray, Jonas realized that sundae was one of the reasons he avoided this place.

Krissy carefully set the tray on the table. She gave Chance his treat: a little plop of doggie-friendly ice cream that Chance inhaled in one gulp.

And then came the surprise: she unloaded the rest of the tray, putting the strawberry milkshake in front of him. She took the sundae, and then slid into the seat across from him.

She saluted him with the spoon. "Let's get to know each other," she said.

She dug into that sundae with approximately the same enthusiasm that Chance had used for his treat.

"This is so good."

The memory came, sharper.

His silence made her look up. "Is something wrong?" Krissy asked him.

Jonas could say no. And he should say no. And yet, he thought of her sharing her confidences with him.

He was shocked how much he wanted to tell her this, as if it was a burden he had carried, long and alone, and he needed to set it down.

He took a tentative sip of the milkshake. He could see why Krissy loved it so. It was rich and creamy, and the taste of strawberries was as magical and uncomplicated as a summer afternoon.

"Are you okay?" she asked again. She set down her spoon.

"Just memories," he said.

"But good ones, right?"

He lifted a shoulder. "Bittersweet, I guess. There was never much money growing up.

The resort and the dogs were a living for our family, but just. The heyday of the kind of resort they showed in *Dirty Dancing* was well over. So we didn't get much in the way of extras. It was a big treat to come here. A once a year event, usually as our season was winding down.

"I never realized until I was in my teens that my Mom always ordered the cheapest thing on the menu.

"So I brought her here the Mother's Day that I was sixteen. My driver's license was pretty freshly minted in my pocket. I didn't let her order. I bought her that."

He nodded toward the mountain of whipped cream and chocolate sauce and ice cream melting in front of Krissy.

"She tried to smile, but she got these tears in her eyes. I guess there's a day when a mother realizes maybe, just maybe, her kids are going to turn out all right. She was just so pleased. She ate every bite.

"Looking back, it seems so small. And too late. Why didn't I see sooner how much she gave and how little she asked in return?

"Her and my dad died in the winter of that year. A car accident on a slippery road. People say funny things after a tragedy like that.

Things like what a blessing that they went together. They loved each other so much."

For a moment, he could not trust himself to speak. "But me and Theresa loved them that much, too. Theresa managed to turn everything they gave us into a gift. She has a life much like the one we experienced as children."

"But you never got over it."

Her words were so quiet.

"No," he admitted, "never. I told myself for the longest time that becoming responsible for Theresa so young made me allergic to being responsible for another person."

"But that isn't it, is it?"

It was unnerving that she got him so completely.

"You love so deeply," she said softly. "So deeply."

And Jonas knew that was it exactly. He had experienced the kind of pain that came from losing someone you loved that much. "I'm not sure I could survive another loss like that."

He glanced up at her. Her eyes were dark and wide, filled with an ache for him that was soothing rather than embarrassing, that made him glad he had confided in her, rather than regretful. Of course, because of her close relationship with her aunt, she would understand like few others would.

After a long time, Krissy nodded. "So here we are," she said. "A match made in heaven. Two people who have experienced the terrible pain of love in very different ways, but with the same result. Sworn off it. Forever."

"Forever," he agreed.

She took a bite of her sundae. For someone sworn off love, he felt inordinately aware of her lips.

He took a sip of his shake. For someone sworn off love, she seemed inordinately focused on his mouth.

She looked away first. They finished their ice cream treats in silence, with eyes skittering everywhere but on each other.

On the walk home, it occurred to him the excursion had been a success only in one area. Chance was coming along nicely.

But really, if the goal was convincing Theresa and Mike this thing was real, there were other issues they should have tackled.

They stopped outside of her cottage.

"Are you still game for this?" he asked her.

"More than ever," Krissy said firmly, as if sharing confidences had strengthened the agreement rather than sending it galloping off in unexpected directions.

"We need to start filling in some blanks," he said, meaning they needed to get it back on track. And that didn't mean sharing vulnerabilities. They needed to stick to the facts!

"How about if I pick you up for dinner Friday night?" he suggested.

"Maybe we could meet in New York? I only work half a day on Fridays, and I was going to go finish up some things at my aunt's office."

"That's perfect. I have a great place in mind."

Krissy considered that. Jonas would know all the great places. Of course he would. Did she even have the right dress for a great place in New York? Was she really already worried about that? Yes!

"I'll pick you up from your aunt's office around six. Bring a list of questions."

"What kind of questions?" she asked.

"You know. Filling-in-the-blanks kind of questions. Knowing-a-person kind of questions. Who was your best friend growing up? What was your dog's name? What was your favorite subject in high school? That kind of thing."

"Okay," she said, but the funny thing was

she felt like she already knew quite a lot about Jonas without having any of those kinds of questions answered. He was a man who would take hours out of his life to drive someone home on a dark night. He was a man who could make a dog mind, firm and gentle by turns. He was a man who had suffered horribly at the hands of fate, and—despite what he said—he had not allowed it to make him hard or bitter.

"You have a bit of chocolate, right…" He touched her lip.

They stood staring at each other for a long time. Long enough that Krissy was well aware that knowing a person had nothing to do with who their best friend was growing up!

He jerked his hand away from her lip, which was a good thing, because she had nearly nibbled it.

It wasn't until he had driven away that Krissy realized he was right. How very little she knew about Jonas. She hadn't even thought to ask him what he did for a living! This fact-finding dinner was a great idea. Essential.

She touched her lip. Good grief! Was it? A woman could redefine what she thought essential was around a man like that!

* * *

Late Friday afternoon, Krissy stood in the middle of her aunt's office. She glanced at the clock. It was time to get ready for Jonas. She took one last look around the office.

Finally, all the phone calls had been made, all the files had been closed, all the boxes had been packed. A mover would come, pick everything up and schedule a delivery for a later date when they could combine several deliveries to Sunshine Cove into one. Thankfully, there was a basement under the cottage where she could store this stuff when it finally arrived.

It should have been a relief to finally have this looked after, all these loose ends tied up. Despite the fact June was a busy month for her, with school also winding up, she was ahead of the end-of-the-month deadline for clearing her aunt's office.

She had given notice to the landlord. But instead of feeling relieved, Krissy felt oddly deflated as it hit her she would never come to this office again.

Match Made in Heaven was no more. Her aunt's life mission—to bring lasting happiness through the discovery of love—was no more.

Krissy slipped into the small washroom.

Hanging on the back of the door was the perfect little black dress.

She shucked her dusty work clothes and slid the dress over her head, and added a hint of makeup, and finally a simple pair of black pumps and a strand of pearls.

She could feel her eyes misting with tears as she snapped on the pearls her aunt had also given her. She remembered the particular excursion where she had gotten this dress. When Krissy had put it on, they had both known it was special, a kind of a once-in-a-lifetime dress that was so "go anywhere" flattering and so feminine—and breathtakingly expensive.

Aunt Jane, who loved shopping, and loved clothes, had insisted on buying it. She had bought the strand of pearls the same day.

No more Match Made in Heaven, no more shopping with her aunt. So many endings. Krissy burst into tears just as a knock came at the back door. Her eyes flew to her watch. She hadn't even done anything with her hair, yet. Not that it mattered. Her makeup was now a mess.

She dabbed at her eyes, and the piece of tissue came away black. The knock came again.

Obviously, everything had changed. She went and opened the back door a crack.

"I came to the back," Jonas said. "I didn't want to set off the alarm."

"I think we should postpone," she said. "I'm not feeling up to it.

"What's wrong?"

"I can't go. I'm sorry. I just—"

He gently shoved the door open and came inside. He gazed down at her. "Krissy?"

"It's over," she wailed. "Match Made in Heaven. Shopping with my aunt."

"I'm sorry," he said.

"Aunt Jane bought me this dress. I said it was silly. I taught kindergarten. I needed wash-and-wear. I need comfortable, durable clothes that can go in the laundry. I might have even mentioned the forbidden polyester word.

"When I tried on this dress, she told me I looked like Audrey Hepburn in *Breakfast at Tiffany's*. She said it didn't matter if I taught kindergarten. I needed to know what the perfect dress felt like."

He took her shoulders and looked at her gravely. "You do," he said. "You look like Audrey Hepburn in *Breakfast at Tiffany's*."

"You probably don't even know who Audrey Hepburn is," she sniffed.

"My mom was a huge fan."

"We just loved each other so much," Krissy said. "I didn't like shopping, but with her, I just basked in her enjoyment of it. Anyway, now I'm a mess. I can't wear this dress without feeling heartbroken, so our date is off."

"Okay," he said soothingly.

"Besides, I look like a raccoon."

"I'll call the restaurant and cancel our reservation."

"I do look like a raccoon, don't I?"

Jonas stepped in close to her. He took his thumb and gently wiped mascara from beneath her eye. It was a useless effort, because the tears began to slide again.

He sighed, and his arms wrapped around her. His scent, so rich, so masculine, somehow so familiar, wrapped around her. It felt like a homecoming.

But that's what she had to remember. Home was the biggest illusion of all. The only thing she'd ever had that was even close to it was the love of her aunt, and now that was gone, too.

Krissy pushed away from him reluctantly. "You should cancel that reservation."

He nodded and took his phone from his pocket. He scrolled through and touched a button. She could hear the phone ringing on the other end.

"Why don't we get takeout?" he said. "We'll take it to the park. Oh, hi. I had a reservation. I have to—"

He looked at her. He smiled, that kind of hopeful smile that he had used when he wanted ice cream.

Note to self: Jonas Boyden, pretty much irresistible at any time, but when he gave you the charming smile? Hopeless.

She nodded.

"—change it to a takeout order. Surprise me. Dinner for two. Allergies?"

He looked over at her. She shook her head.

"No allergies. I need plates and cutlery, too. Pull out all stops," he said. "I'm trying to impress a girl who looks exactly like Audrey Hepburn." He paused. "That's no object."

He disconnected and looked at the phone, pleased. "There's an item off my list already."

"List?"

"The get-to-know-each-other list? Allergies. None."

"Well, penicillin, but they hardly ever add that to food."

Despite her deliberate effort to keep her tone light, his mentioning the list was a reminder what this was really about. Getting to know each other for fake mate purposes. She hadn't expected it to be so much like a doctor's appointment. She had thought it might be more personal.

"I'll just go change," she said. It wasn't 100

percent social. She should have remembered that when she put on this dress in the first place. It was like a job interview, only in reverse, since she already had the job.

This was a dress a woman wore when she wanted to get to know someone in a different way. A way that had nothing to do with allergies!

"Don't you dare."

She was going to tell him it was no more practical to wear this dress on a picnic than it would be to teach kindergarten.

But somehow the words never came out of her mouth. It wasn't just the look on his face, either, though his look made it clear this wasn't 100 percent like an interview for him, either, even if that was what he wanted it to be.

It was as if her aunt was giving her yet another gift: not just the dress, but an ability to be open to life's surprises.

Jonas wasn't dressed for a picnic, either, but for dinner at one of New York's finest restaurants. He looked completely at home in a dark charcoal suit and knife-pressed narrow slacks. The brilliant shirt looked—and had felt—like silk. The tie was also dark charcoal, with a raised pattern of darker swirls on it. The pocket square was a perfect, slender rectangle of white.

"I'll just go wash my face," Krissy said.

An hour later, Jonas had purchased a blanket and they had picked up the food from a restaurant that Krissy recognized as a New York hot spot, where it was nearly impossible to get a reservation. They made their way into Central Park.

He set out the blanket on the gentle slope of Cherry Hill, overlooking Bow Bridge. A confetti of finished pink petals drifted on the ground like snow.

Krissy sat down, thinking she would feel awkward, but no, she tucked her legs to one side and watched as Jonas got rid of the jacket, then the tie, tossing them casually on the blanket and then sitting down, stretching his legs out in front of him.

He began to take items out of the basket. She understood suddenly exactly what he had meant when he'd said, *"That's no object."*

Money, obviously.

"Did they give you *real* plates?"

"So it appears. And, look, *real* wine-glasses."

"We're not allowed to drink alcohol in Central Park!"

"Oh, well, they put in a bottle of wine." He

looked at it. "A very good bottle, too. And glasses, so we'll live dangerously this once."

"Somehow, I don't think living dangerously is a one-off for you."

For some reason, that made her look at his lips. And suddenly living dangerously felt altogether too enticing!

CHAPTER TEN

"ME LIVING DANGEROUSLY?" Jonas wagged his eyebrows at her. "It seems to me it's you who has nearly gotten us arrested before, not me."

"How do you figure that? It wasn't me knocking on the door in the middle of the night."

"It wasn't exactly the middle of the night. And I did have an appointment."

Krissy enjoyed this teasing, the back-and-forth banter, more than she should have. The setting was just so lovely, the evening light perfect, warmth in the air. A young couple went by in a rowboat, him putting his muscle into moving the boat, her trailing her hand in the water. She splashed him, and their laughter drifted up the hill.

"Remember you asked me if I'd ever done kid things?" she asked him. "How funny we would end up here today. My aunt brought me here once. We rented one of the rowboats. I think that was exactly her intention, to do a 'kid' activity with me."

"And how was it?"

Krissy laughed. "You would have to know my aunt better than you did to know how funny it was. She had on high heels and a Chanel suit. She loved crazy hats and she had on this huge sunbonnet. She tried to row the boat, and she kept going in circles. So then we changed places and nearly capsized the boat. The wind came up and took her hat off, and we chased it all over the reservoir. She nearly fell in half a dozen times reaching to get the hat. Every time her fingers would touch it, it would drift away. I feel like I can hear her laughing now. Even though the hat was ruined by the time we did retrieve it, and we were both sunburned and exhausted, she said it was the best day ever."

"What a great memory," he said warmly.

Jonas finished unpacking the bag: beautiful white cardboard boxes came out, one by one, each with a handwritten label. *Baked Brie with Pecans. Mixed Green Salad with Dates and Goat Cheese. Smoked Crab with Herbed Crème Fraîche. Assorted Dessert.* With a sigh of surrender, Krissy realized it was exactly the kind of meal one would eat in this kind of dress.

He handed her a plate and an appetizer, then put wine in one of the tall, long-stemmed glasses.

"Cheers," he said, and lifted his glass to her.

Somehow, as their glasses clinked and their eyes met over the rims, she knew her aunt would approve of her christening the dress like this.

"Here's to getting to know each other," he said, reminding her that there was a mission, after all. He pulled a list out of his wallet, carefully unfolded it and set it down on the blanket. He took a pen out of his breast pocket and wrote something down.

"What did you write?"

"Knows her way around a rowboat," he said, and the laughter leaped up between them, easy and comfortable.

Krissy took a bite of the Brie. It was incredible.

"I don't even know what you do for a living," she said. "I mean aside from the fact it involves lawyers and owning all the hotels on the Monopoly board."

Jonas laughed. "I own a company called Last Resort. Basically, I buy properties that are run-down or struggling or both, bring them up to standard, put an operational plan in place, run them until they're making money again and then flip them."

"That's an interesting business."

"I was born for it. I mentioned to you our family resort was pretty hand-to-mouth. When my parents died, there was an insurance policy. I took a chance that I could turn it around. I looked around at all the failing resorts in the Catskills and tried to figure out what to do differently. What would make people come back for that kind of vacation?

"I started researching to see what people wanted when they were looking for a place to have a vacation.

"The hardest issue for them to resolve seemed to be pets. People wanted to holiday with Rover, and resorts did not want pets. And so we became the first pet-friendly resort in our area. I brought the cabins up to a new standard, including dog bath stations outside each one. That first time, I hired Mike, and we did all the work ourselves. And then Theresa and I worked on dog-focused programs like weeklong obedience immersion."

"I'd take that!" Krissy said.

"Exactly. We found a niche people wanted. We made our motto Dog-Gone Fun. My sister loved it—loves it—and was content with it, but I was bored within a year. About the same time Theresa had produced the first little monster. I noticed troubling changes in her. One day, she said to me, *'I always thought I'd be a yummy mommy.'* She went on to say she felt fat and frumpy and like she always had some mystery smudge on the front of her blouse. She said she had days when she didn't know whether to eat lunch or have a shower. Sometimes Mike came home from work, and she realized she hadn't even combed her hair. The resort next door to ours had been boarded up for years, so I went and took a look. I was thinking a health and wellness of some sort, but after talking to my sister, I wanted to target her demographic. So I picked young moms. I revamped the whole place so it had a very spa-like aesthetic. We developed hour, day and weeklong retreats that focused on delicious food, quiet spaces, learning yoga or meditation or music or art. A mom could have a facial or a massage or a long walk or a soak. And then Theresa figured out the thing that really sold it: child care. Moms might not like the day in, day out drudgery of their kids, but they aren't going to leave them for any length of time, either. We called it Yummy Mommy."

"I've heard of that!" In fact, Krissy's coworker, fifth grade teacher Martha Montrose, went every year.

"I sold the majority of the ownership a few months in. I realized my strength was in the concept, but the operational side bored me. And then I went on to the next one. I keep a percentage, I move on. I think I'm over a hundred properties in right now."

"So you do own all the hotels on the game board!"

He laughed. "Working on it."

"And you have no formal training in any of this? No university? No degree?"

"No, I kind of plunged right into the working world and all these massive projects when I was eighteen and never looked back."

"You know what I like the best? That it's about your family. The first one about saving your family business, and then the second one was about seeing a need in your sister. It's about love for you, isn't it?"

He cleared his throat uncomfortably. "Love and business don't mix."

"I think you're amazing." She blushed. "I mean, that's amazing."

Jonas laughed, obviously trying to keep it light. "That's exactly what we want—my fiancée to think I'm amazing. In fact—" he took his phone out of his pocket "—I'm going to take a picture of you looking amazed at me."

"Just a sec." She picked up her wineglass. "Here's to the amazing Jonas." Just as he took the picture she crossed her eyes and stuck out her tongue. "Post that on Instagram."

"I actually don't use social media," he said, still holding up his phone. As soon as she uncrossed her eyes and tucked her tongue back in her mouth, he took another picture. "The company does, and I have a specialist who puts together posts, but I don't have any personal accounts. I don't get the concept of living your life as if it's an open book, seeing every event as a photo op to be posted instead of something just to be enjoyed. This is a great pic."

He turned his phone to her and showed her both photos. The one was quite hilarious, but the other one had a loveliness to it she found startling. She had scrubbed all her makeup off and had never gotten around to doing anything with her hair. Still, there was something about the photo she really liked. There was an expression on her face she didn't see often.

She looked relaxed. Happy. With a faint undertone of hopefulness. Or maybe it was wistfulness.

"Do you do social media?" Jonas asked her. "You want a copy of it?"

She did want a copy of whatever he had captured that she usually did not see in herself, though in all fairness, she did not see many pictures of herself.

"No, send it to my phone. I don't do social media, either. Mostly because of the teaching thing. Even though some teachers use it with a false name, I just don't want my kids—or their parents—snooping around in my life."

"We have something in common!" he crowed. He picked up his crumpled list off the blanket and pretended to write on it. "No social media. The fact that I don't even have your phone number yet shows this is quite an old-fashioned kind of romance. My sister will approve."

It was a much-needed reminder that this old-fashioned romance was really not a romance at all—a hard thing to keep in mind with the delicious food and the wine, and the growing ease of being with him. A hard thing to keep in mind when he talked about his sister.

It was the same as when he had talked about his mom.

He might protest; he might say otherwise, but Jonas was the rarest of things: a decent guy. She could feel herself falling just a little bit in love with him.

A little bit in love with him? She should watch the wine! He seemed to be topping her glass up more than his own. In fact, he might still be sipping his first one.

"I think I'll send her this picture, kind of a little foreshadowing of what's to come."

"Foreshadowing," she said wryly. "A literary term. Do you like to read, then?"

"Love it. Nothing literary, though. Espionage, suspense."

"Me, too. Murder and mayhem."

Just like that, it was so easy. The food and the wine disappeared as they talked about favorite books and favorite movies, favorite things they had done and planned to do. They talked about childhood friends and pets, naturally, no lists involved.

Jonas, now stretched out, leaning on his side on one elbow, finally flicked open the lid on the dessert box.

She peered in. "Wow."

"They're all individually labeled. Look at this one." He held up a fragile delicacy for her to look at.

She leaned in closer and read the lovely miniature sign that had been planted in the dessert on a toothpick. "Buttermilk panna cotta with raspberry and rose."

"There's only one of each," he said. He teased her by opening his mouth as if he was going to gobble up the whole thing.

She grabbed his wrist, and they pretended to struggle.

"One of the first things I teach in kindergarten is the value of sharing," she said, and then she leaned in, and bit half the dessert right out of his hand. There was a spot of the glaze on the mound below his pointer finger. She blamed what happened next on the wine.

Jonas felt Krissy's lips touch his hand. And then he felt just the faintest flick of her tongue. The intensity of it felt like a burn. Like a brand.

He snatched his hand away and managed to avoid looking at it to see if there was a mark. He popped the rest of the treat in his mouth. She had closed her eyes and was rolling the confection over her tongue. A little sigh of pure pleasure escaped her as she swallowed. Awareness of her burned in him, more scorching than the brand of her tongue.

She opened her eyes and gazed at him with sudden, unveiled hunger that could not be satiated with dessert.

The sensual tension leaping between them was at least as delightful and at least as delicious as the dessert selection. He took another confection from the box and held it out to her, hoping for a barrier, knowing it was an invitation.

Which she accepted. She nibbled. Her breath tickled his hand. She had icing sugar on her lip.

He had, truth be told, done quite a bit of dating in his day.

Bimbos, Krissy's aunt had proclaimed scornfully.

But still bimbos who knew their way around the art of pleasing a man. And yet, there was something about this—sitting on a blanket on a warm evening with flower petals floating around them—that was infinitely more powerful than just about anything he had ever experienced.

His mouth was dry. His heart was pounding. She reached out with the tip of her tongue and flicked that speck of icing sugar away from her lip. It scorched him nearly as badly as when she had flicked her tongue to his hand.

Her lips were moist and plump. He wanted to taste her. He wanted to do exactly the same thing he had done when there had been chocolate on her lip the other afternoon.

She blinked at him. Her lips parted faintly. The desire that had sprung up over dessert was mutual. Really, this particular spring storm had been coming between them since the first time they had touched, and it had been building like thunderclouds on the horizon.

Jonas leaned in closer yet to Krissy. One part of his brain tried to remind him that this arrangement between them was going to be complicated enough.

But another part assured him that he couldn't very well fake an engagement without any physical contact.

Better to do it now, his rational mind whispered, in somewhat controlled circumstances. It wouldn't do to be taken totally by surprise by kissing her for the first time in front of Theresa or Mike.

It was like a practice run—that was all.

But when Jonas's lips touched Krissy's, there was nothing about it that was controlled, nothing about it that felt like a practice run, absolutely nothing about it that was for the benefit of convincing his sister of something at some faraway future date.

In fact, those things were wiped from his mind. Completely. Except the part about it being a total surprise.

Even though he had seen hints of passion sparking in her eyes, nothing could have prepared him for this part of her.

Krissy tasted of wine. And of the desserts they had just eaten. But she also tasted of mystery and the unknown, of all that was feminine and of the secret powers of the universe. She was *Breakfast at Tiffany's* but she was also a fresh mountain morning with mist rising off a lake. She was a perfect bouquet of roses and she was a wildflower meadow. She was innocence, and she was seduction.

She was a model, an actress, a queen. She was an Olympian and a warrior. She was as complex and multifaceted as a diamond and as simple, as of the earth, as a fresh-turned shovel of soil. In her was that same ripe promise of being able to give life.

"Oh," she said softly, breaking the contact of their lips, but staying close enough that she could taste him again in a heartbeat. Her eyes were wide and dazed on his face.

It occurred to him, that she might have consumed most of the wine. Which made this totally wrong, as if it wasn't totally wrong, anyway.

Jonas was glad they were in a park in such a public setting. Because if this had happened the other night outside her door, there was no telling where it would have led.

He got to his feet and stretched mightily before she could lean into him again. Before he leaned into her again. He began to gather up the picnic things from around her. "It's getting late. I'll take you home."

To that front door, where the options were going to be so much different.

He had an hour's drive, he told himself sternly, to gird his loins for the coming battle, to pull himself together. It was not as if he was a callow boy incapable of saying no to temptation.

She got up off the blanket. Her hair was wild and curly, and her dress was rumpled, as if they had done quite a bit more than share a kiss. She was stiff from sitting for so long. She stretched, hands way up over her head, dress riding high up the long delicate curve of her thigh.

"You don't have to take me home," she said. "You can just drop me at the train."

Uh-huh, like he was going to put her on a train looking like that.

She followed his gaze and smoothed her dress. "I could go back to my aunt's office and get changed."

"It's okay. I don't mind the drive."

"Should you be driving? How much have you had to drink?" she asked.

"Quite a bit less than you." In fact, he was not even sure he had finished an entire glass of wine. She, however, with those flushed cheeks and starry eyes, was demonstrating every sign of slight inebriation. Another reason not to put her on the train. She giggled, confirmation of how much less than her he had had.

"I'd like to see Chance, anyway," he said, heading further argument off at the pass.

She smiled at him as if he had declared they shared a beautiful child.

Something happened to Jonas that had never happened to him before. Not ever. He wondered what a child they made together would look like.

It was the most astonishing—and terrifying—thought he'd ever had.

Because here was the thing: Jonas Boyden was *not* a baby kind of guy. His nephews, in that baby stage, had been cute, but messy and demanding. He had watched Theresa's transformation—and Mike's to a lesser extent—from once-intelligent people, now given to discussing what a crayon that had passed through a digestive system looked like. It had been the start of Yummy Mommy but had killed any other parenting ambitions Jonas had, admittedly slight as those had been to begin with.

He made the mistake of glancing at Krissy again, and remembered what he had tasted on her lips: the ripe ability to give life.

He was suddenly so aware, looking at her, that it was what she needed, and probably what she desired, deep down in that secret place, a place protected by the barbwire fence of the hurts inflicted on her by her family.

But Jonas was willing to bet it was those hidden longings that had led her to teach kindergarten. It was those hidden longings that had made her so susceptible to Chance's debatable charm.

She *needed.*

She needed love and stability and something to care about, even as she denied needing those things.

Jonas was self-aware enough to know he was not the man to entrust with those kinds of needs.

And yet still, he now was tangled enough with her to want things for her. To want to change her mind about family, so that she could have what she secretly wanted and what she surely deserved.

A family of her own.

A good family.

Family the way it should be. That safe place. That solid place. That soft place to fall in a hard, hard world.

And there was nobody more qualified to show her what family really was than his own. So, as dangerous as this had become, Jonas felt more committed to getting her to that family reunion than ever. She could just never know it had become about so much more than keeping his car.

He had an hour, he told himself, to get this thing back on an even keel. To get things back on track.

He disposed of the rubbish and put the blanket over his arm. She hesitated for just a moment and then tossed her hair—the woman warrior—and took his hand in hers as if she owned it, as if their hands belonged together.

Such a simple thing, the intertwining of hands.

So why was it Jonas was no longer even sure where the track was, never mind how to get back on it?

CHAPTER ELEVEN

KRISSY FELL ASLEEP on the way home. She was horrified when she woke up as Jonas pulled his sleek car to a gliding halt in front of her house, aware there was a little pool of drool darkening her dress.

She was even more horrified when the memory of that kiss came back to her.

"Oh," she said. "I don't drink very much. It went straight to my head." She scrambled out of the car and headed down the walk.

The wine had made her forget the most important aspect of all this: *it wasn't real.* How could it not be real? Jonas's lips claiming hers had felt like one of the most real experiences of her entire life.

Which, she told herself firmly, spoke to a pathetic life.

She fumbled for her key. Jonas was behind her.

"I guess we shouldn't kiss anymore," she said, as brightly as she could.

"Really? I think it was good to get it over with. You know, before we have an audience. So we both know what to expect."

Get it over with? Know what to expect?

Well, no one should know better than her the value of a good experiment. Still, Krissy had obviously made a complete fool of herself.

"Well, good," she managed to say. "Lots accomplished tonight. I think we've gotten to know each other quite well enough."

"Do you?" he said.

She opened the door, and Chance bounded out, went right past her, his new Frisbee caught between his teeth. He sat in front of Jonas, his tail thumping the ground and his tongue lolling out, begging for just one toss.

"What a good dog," Jonas said.

The dog quivered ecstatically, but did not leap up.

Jonas got down on his haunches in front of the dog and did that massage thing to that huge marred face.

So every living thing felt the chemistry of this man, every living thing longed to be more to him, every living thing longed to feel the warmth of his approval.

"I think we could consider the dress rehearsal over," she said. "If you think of any other details about yourself that I need to know, text me. I'll do the same. And the family reunion. Do we have a plan? Drop by on it for a few hours? Announce our engagement? Look besotted with each other? Leave?"

"Ah, maybe not quite that easy. They'll expect us to stay the weekend."

The dog moaned his happiness and pushed his ear deeper into Jonas's hand. He nearly lost his grip on the Frisbee but managed to keep it from falling from his jaws. It was quite distracting.

"Together?" Did her voice have a faintly hysterical shriek to it?

"Well, yeah, but the cottages are quite large. No one will know if I take the couch. Except maybe you, eh, Chance?"

Aside from the dog, she would know. And after what happened tonight, it just seemed like a really lousy idea to share close quarters with him while they were pretending for his family.

That was her lesson from tonight. She sucked at pretending.

"Maybe we could tell them I have a belief system that precludes sharing accommodations with you?" she suggested.

He looked skeptical.

"I don't look like that kind of girl? I mean, it needn't be overt. I wouldn't carry a hymnal. Or start preaching at the campfire. A small gold cross around my neck. An occasional softly murmured, *praise be.*"

For somebody who sucked at pretending, Krissy realized she was getting into this.

Probably because it was making Jonas laugh. It was an absolute weakness to enjoy making him laugh so much. Which was why they had to call it quits on the dress rehearsals.

"I actually think," Jonas said, cocking his head at her and standing up, though his hand still rested on Chance's head, "you've shown yourself to be more the warrior type. Plus, uh, I'm not sure my sister would ever be convinced that I would go for a Goody Two-shoes kind of gal."

"I am a Goody Two-shoes kind of gal!"

"Not really," he said softly.

"Joan of Arc was a warrior *and* a girl of strong conviction. You better believe she wasn't sharing a cottage with her betrothed."

"Did she have a betrothed?" That gorgeous, sexy smile tickled his lips. "So you're thinking of going in costume, now?"

"Thinking of it," she said solemnly. "We could shop for a sword instead of a ring."

"Chain mail should do the trick if we end up sharing a cottage," he said thoughtfully, his smile deepening wickedly. So he knew sharing a cottage was going to be a challenge for both of them! But it seemed to be one he was anticipating with some delight.

She snapped her finger and thumb together. "Okay, forget Joan."

"As hard as that will be," he said, his tone solemn, but still smiling.

"This is better, and more practical. I'll get a call that there's been some sort of emergency. I'll have to leave."

"Maybe we should just play it by ear," he said. "Come prepared for the weekend, and if you're uncomfortable, we'll pull the plug. But I actually think you'll like it."

That was the problem. She liked playing Cinderella to his Prince Charming just a little too much.

"Chance will love it out there." He took his phone out of his pocket and took a picture of the dog mooning at him adoringly.

Argh! Get to her through the dog!

"And there's one other thing, since you mentioned it. We have to get you a ring."

"No sword?" Krissy said as lightly as she

could to cover up what a perfectly awful outing shopping for a ring with him would be. She could unfortunately picture Jonas slipping a ring on her finger for this make-believe engagement.

"No sword," he said firmly.

"Oh, sure, then. A ring. Pick whatever you like."

He cocked his head at her. "You aren't a jewelry person at all, are you?"

"Not really."

"The ring should be sized."

How many rings had he bought for people? Was it his favorite bauble to give?

"I mean nothing would alert to a fake engagement like a ring falling off your finger. Do you want to just go pick one soon? Then it will be sized in time for the reunion?"

"I'll check my calendar," she said haughtily.

"Krissy..." He took a step toward her. She was aware how much she had to tilt her head to look at him. She was aware of the jolt right through to her heart when she looked at his lips, when she remembered the intoxicating, weak-to-the-bone sensation of taking them with her own.

"Yes?" Still with the haughty tone.

"You had fun, didn't you?"

The question took her off guard. For some reason, she thought of her aunt's Match Made in Heaven questionnaire.

What do you do for fun?

There was something ever so faintly imploring in Jonas's tone. He liked having fun. He wanted her to have fun.

Was it so evident she was not really a having-fun kind of person?

"Yes," she said, dropping the you-can't-touch-me veneer, and admitting the truth to herself. And to him. "Yes, I had fun."

She remembered her aunt's *Nothing naughty, please* instruction. Maybe that kiss had been the most fun of all, even though it was the playing-with-fire piece. Or maybe it was so much fun because it was thrilling, because it was playing with fire.

Even now, this simple thing, bantering back and forth with him, was fun.

"Can't we just do that?" he asked, his voice low, utterly charming in its beseeching tone. "Can't we just have fun?"

It was an enchantment. Wearing her wonderful dress to the impromptu picnic in Central Park had made her feel like she was Cinderella at the ball.

And Jonas was suggesting that the clock had not struck midnight, and that she didn't have to lose the glass slipper just yet.

He was right. It had been fun. The whole thing was just fun. She had been invited to take part in some good old family high jinks. Jonas wanted to win a bet, and he planned to have fun doing it. No one was going to get hurt. His deep-seated love for his sister was obvious.

Krissy was along for the ride. A roller-coaster ride, obviously, with lots of stomach dropping dips, long climbs of anticipation, tight, hang-on-for-dear-life twists and turns.

For once in her life, Krissy didn't have to be so cautious. Or know the final result. Or plan everything out to a conclusion that would bring her a sense of safety and security. She just had to buckle up and hang on for dear life, didn't she?

"Can you do that?" Jonas asked. "Can you just have some fun with it?"

Suddenly, she felt she wasn't going to be relegated to the stick-in-the-mud who needed carefree Jonas Boyden to bring her to life. She was not going to be the wilting daisy, waiting for him to water her! She was suddenly not prepared to buckle up and hang on for dear life. Let Jonas buckle up and hang on for dear life!

She leaned over and took the Frisbee from Chance. Then she reached up and kissed Jonas full on the lips. Any Goody Two-shoes kind of girl that she had ever been, she now banished firmly.

"So," she called to Jonas, she and Chance already running, "let's do it, then. Let's have some fun."

Jonas hardly even hesitated. He ran after her onto the sprawling, carpet-like lawn of the mansion that neighbored hers. She kicked off her shoes.

"Aren't we trespassing?" he asked her, but he was already kicking off his shoes, too, and peeling off his socks.

"They're hardly ever home. I keep an eye on their place, so I'm pretty sure they'd be okay with it."

Chance begged her for the Frisbee. She threw it to Jonas. It was a terrible throw and he had to run really fast and jump really high to beat Chance to it. He grabbed it out of the air. Really, he looked so magnificent that she saw many bad throws in his future!

He threw it back to her. His throw, naturally, was perfect, and, to the distress of the dog, she snatched it out of the air. She deliberately threw quite wide of Jonas, hoping to see that wonderful demonstration of athleticism again, but this time it was Chance who grabbed it out of the air, ecstatic. They ran after him, and finally—if briefly—retrieved the toy. They played until they were breathless with laughter and exertion.

Finally, they could run no more. Krissy collapsed on the grass first, and Jonas came beside her. The dog was content to lay his big head across Jonas's belly and chew on his Frisbee as Jonas toyed with his ears.

In comfortable silence, they lay in the grass as night chased the last light from the summer sky and the stars winked on, one by one.

Jonas leaned up on one elbow and looked at her.

"You're not drunk, are you?"

"Not even a little bit," she whispered. Maybe she had been. She wasn't sure. But if she was drunk now, it wasn't on wine.

He traced the line of her face with his hand. "I can't stop myself," he said with wonder. He dropped his mouth over hers.

She could not stop herself, either. She welcomed him back to her. His mouth was now both familiar and dangerously unknown.

And then the automatic sprinklers came on.

Jonas leaped off her and held out his hand

to her. Under a star-studded sky, they ran hand in hand through the sprinklers, gathering up their shoes, laughing joyously.

He never let go of her hand. They found themselves at her front door once again. Her dress was plastered to her. His slacks and shirt were plastered to him.

She reached up and touched the droplets on his soaked face and then took them from her fingertips with her lips. He moaned and dropped his head over hers.

She took the moistness of the sprinkler water from the fullness of his lips with her tongue, one droplet at a time. And then he did the same to her.

And then that was not enough. The kiss deepened exquisitely, tortuously. She could feel every muscle of his body tensing beneath the wetness of his clothing, which was not really a barrier at all. Their kiss deepened yet more. With discovery. With exploration. It was exhilaration. With pure ecstasy.

It was life itself that she tasted when she tasted so fully of him. The force of it rippled through him, surged, enveloped her. Some slumbering part of her stirred awake, sputtered to life and then roared like a fire being fed oxygen. She knew this powerful thing unleashed between them could not be put back to sleep again.

"Are you coming in?" Krissy murmured helplessly against the rough whiskers of his cheek. She wanted him. She wanted him as much as she had ever wanted anything—anybody—in her entire life. No, it was not want. It was need. She needed him with the hunger of someone who had been starving; she needed him like a wintered plant needed sunlight to live.

The kiss between them reflected all of that and became ferocious with the tender violence of their mutual need.

He reared back from her, his eyes taking in her face.

"I thought," he reminded her roughly, "you weren't that kind of girl."

"I'm not," she whispered, "but maybe I have always wanted to be. Maybe the right person never came along before."

And then he scooped her soaked body up in his arms, and she felt deliciously consumed by the scorching heat of him. He found the handle and nudged open the door with his foot.

The three of them. Krissy and Jonas tumbled through it, Chance bounding past them into the house.

CHAPTER TWELVE

JONAS WOKE UP the next morning with the dog laid out across the foot of the bed crushing his feet and Krissy nestled against him, her hair scattered, a sheet covering some, but not all, of her curves.

Her hand was resting on his chest—his naked chest. Something sweetly possessive about that.

Looking at her without her awareness, he took in the thick sweep of her lashes, the delicate roundness of cheek and shoulder, the beautiful bow and slight movement of her lips as the breath moved in and out of her.

Jonas felt the searing and shocking memory of what had unfolded, white-hot, between them last night.

But another feeling overlaid that one, and it was more powerful: he felt the most exquisite tenderness for this woman whose sensuous warmth was pressed against him. And he felt enormously protective of her.

They both knew she wasn't that kind of girl. What had she said last night?

That she had always wanted to be. She had proved that in spades: by turns playful, demanding, ferocious, giving, gentle.

It was the second part of her statement that a better man would have paid attention to.

That maybe the right person had never come along before. Jonas was well aware he was no one's *right person*.

He waited for panic to set in, and the self-recrimination. What the hell had he done? He hadn't even been drunk. And neither had she.

But intoxicated, yes. On her laughter. On her wet body in that little black dress pressed against his, on the look in her eyes.

And oh, yes, on the taste of those incredible lips.

But, oddly, no sense of recrimination came.

Krissy stirred and then her eyes opened and then opened wider. She didn't look upset; she looked the very same way he felt.

Happy to be waking up beside him in the same way he felt happy to be waking up beside her, as if something that had been missing from their worlds—without their awareness—was suddenly there.

She came fully awake and was suddenly shy. He couldn't resist cupping her face in his hands and kissing her on the lips with all that tenderness he was feeling toward her.

The dog whined.

"I think he needs to go out," she whispered against Jonas's mouth. "Why don't you take him?" she suggested. "I'll make us some breakfast."

There were many things on his mind besides the dog and breakfast, but she was right to put the brakes on this thing unfolding between them before they were both so swept away with it that not one other rational decision could be made. Hopefully a walk would be a great way to get his head back on straight. He put on his crumpled clothes and went out the door. Instead of getting his head back on straight, Jonas found he couldn't wait to get back to her and couldn't stop thinking about her. He stopped and plucked a flower from a garden that bordered the walk.

When he got back, Krissy was showered and dressed in a pair of yoga pants and an oversize T-shirt. She was very focused on making pancakes. He let the dog off the leash and went up behind her. He wrapped his arms around her and buried his face in the sweet curve of her neck.

When she turned into him, he gave her the flower.

"Oh," she said, blushing crimson, "how lovely!"

That blush reminded him of what he was dealing with. It had been a long, long time since he had been with a woman who blushed.

It was a little late for this, but Jonas realized he needed to take things slowly. He was dealing with grief. He knew from experience how intensely vulnerable she was right now. He should just give her—and himself—some space.

"We should—"

She turned and looked at him, and he saw what she was expecting in the sudden vulnerability of her expression.

If he asked for space right now, she would not see it as being for the greater good of both of them. She would see it as a brush-off.

"We should go get that ring today," he heard himself say.

What? a voice inside him asked, shocked.

"What?" she asked, shocked.

"There's a jewelry store in a little town north of here. It's close to one of my favorite hiking trails. Have you got sturdy boots?"

* * *

Krissy stared at Jonas.

He'd brought her a flower. Snatched from someone's garden, but a romantic gesture nonetheless.

Now he wanted to go ahead with the ring? The whole time she had cooked breakfast she had thought he would arrive back with the dog and a zillion reasons to bolt out of here.

She had a zillion reasons she needed him to leave. This was all becoming exactly as he had predicted! Terribly complex.

For instance, she couldn't even look at him without wanting to touch him, kiss him, drag him back down the hall… Shop for a ring when she was feeling some dangerous hope zinging in the air between them. Wouldn't that be utter madness?

Still, he had put ring shopping into perspective really quickly. For him, the ring shopping was a casual outing—it had nothing at all to do with what had transpired between them last night. In fact, it could combine with a hike! Sturdy boots, indeed!

That was the proper outlook.

"Can I use your shower?" he asked. "And maybe pop my clothes into the dryer for a bit to loosen the wrinkles?"

Krissy gulped.

Jonas Boyden had been in her bed. Now he was going to be in *her* shower. Part of her longed to be as bold as she had been last night and get in that shower with him.

But another part of her held back. *They barely knew one another.* Wasn't this how her parents had gotten into such difficulties? They had hurried into a relationship when they didn't even understand each other's core values. Their legacy had been that Krissy grew up fast and learned to depend on herself from a very young age.

She had to take this lesson now and back this thing up. It felt as if it would be way too easy to start depending on Jonas. Already, her safe and tidy little cottage felt as if it would never be the same, as if some part of Jonas would linger here tantalizingly, so could you go backward once you had gone *there*?

She heard the shower turn on. She imagined the water sluicing over that gorgeous body that she had owned last night. But then she also heard the dryer thumping.

Was this a man who was accustomed to waking up in a strange bed? He seemed very practiced at getting wrinkles out of clothes that had been left in a hurried heap by the side of the bed.

Tell him to go home, Krissy ordered herself. But already she wasn't that strong; already she was prepared to ignore the lessons life had given her. She wanted to spend the day with him. She wanted to see where all this was going to go.

No doubt, straight to a heartbreak, she warned herself. But even with that warning inside her head, while he was still showering, she quickly chose a suitable hiking outfit: a pair of denim shorts and a plaid shirt. She braided her hair.

Then she looked at herself in the mirror, hoping she had achieved a nice, casual outdoorsy image. Good grief. A little too Daisy Mae? But it was too late; she could hear him emerge from the shower.

He came out of the bathroom with a towel tucked around his waist and water beaded in the strands of his hair, turned dark gold from water. Her helpless eyes trailed to the perfect, muscled body.

He paused and looked at her. He smiled. "Hey, you look awesome in braids. Very wholesome."

A reminder to them both that they were in totally different leagues?

He got his clothes out of the dryer and put them on. It was his business attire from yesterday—minus the suit jacket—and yet he looked like a poster boy for an outdoor excursion being featured in *Men's Fitness*. There was nothing Li'l Abner about him, except maybe for the broadness of his shoulders.

Considering what had occurred between them last night, did she want to look wholesome? Considering that, wasn't it the safest thing? Considering their mission today—an engagement ring—wasn't it a good thing he was setting the tone by treating the hike as the main event?

Soon Chance was loaded into the back hatch. The dog was over the moon to be having an outing with them.

As they took to the highway, Krissy felt some tension leaving her. It was that perfect kind of day that only late June had: warmth without too much heat, the crispness of summer, spring freshness still in the air, the world bright green with growth and lushness that sang of possibility.

The vehicle filled with the heady scent of his shower-washed body.

He glanced at her, smiled that smile that made her feel cherished, as if she *mattered* to him. "Cat got your tongue, Krissy?"

She didn't think any talk of tongues was a very good idea right now!

"Tell me something wonderful about your

week," he said to her, and she loved it that he had sensed her awkwardness and was prepared to work at easing it.

Well, there was the picnic. And then there was something quite wonderful crowding out all the other wonderfuls.

"Something I don't know about," he said softly, reading her mind. "Maybe something from work."

So Krissy found herself telling him about Georgie, her very adorable five-year-old class miscreant.

"He brought worms for show-and-tell. Then he chased Emily all over the class with one. I think it's the five-year-old way of saying I like you. But then, when I told him to lose the worm, he ate it. I think his chances with Emily are over for good now."

"Note to self—don't eat worms in front of the girl you are trying to impress."

Krissy gulped. Was *that* girl her? "I think you're way past the eating worms stage of impressing a girl," she said. She thought of his mouth. *Way* past.

"You are way overestimating the sophistication of the male species," he said, and the laughter that rose up between them was deliciously comfortable and companionable.

"What about you?" she asked. "Best part of your week."

He gave her a lazy, sexy smile that turned her insides to mush and made her happily aware there was no question about what had been best about his week.

"I acquired a resort about a year ago that's been an extraordinary challenge. It's in the Florida Keys, more run-down than we thought it was going to be. Usually, I have a pretty good sense of how the resort will feel specialized, but for this one every single thing about it has been a grind, including the mission statement. But it all came together last week. I haven't run a resort in conjunction with a charity before, but one of my executives is a military veteran, and he was telling me about some of the challenges military families have during—and sometimes especially after—their service.

"So we're going to work with veteran's groups, and provide getaways for these really stressed and sometimes not very well off families."

Krissy could not even look at him. She was sure the admiration she had for him—the growing sense of connection, the desire to know this man, completely, to be a part of his life—would just be too evident in her face.

"You should come," he said after a moment, "to the opening."

She nearly quivered with pure longing. He had just opened the door to a future beyond this, and beyond the weekend with his family.

"Wouldn't that be, um, kind of complicated?" she asked, trying to strip the helpless sense of longing from her voice. "It would mean extending the charade, wouldn't it?"

They needed to address that. Didn't they? The charade part?

She was hoping he would say it wasn't a charade, not anymore. But he didn't.

He frowned. He sighed. "Yes." And then almost to himself, "It's not as if I didn't see it coming. Complications."

The silence between them did not seem comfortable anymore.

The town that was their destination was a village, much like Sunshine Cove, only smaller. The day was cool enough to leave Chance in the vehicle with all the windows open, but now that they were actually in front of the tiny jewelry store, sandwiched in between a bookshop and an antique store, Krissy felt reluctant to go in.

"Are you sure you want to leave the vehicle unsecured?" Krissy said. She suddenly did not want to do this. It was too personal. Too crazy. Too much a lie. There was too much potential to feel things she did not want to feel. Especially after last night.

Like her growing attachment to Jonas. There was this sense in her of wanting to know him so completely. And that was without the further complication of the fact that she couldn't look at his lips without thinking of kissing him. Of his hands claiming her. Of her hands exploring him. Like how much she enjoyed making him laugh.

How could she possibly go look at a ring with Jonas—an engagement ring—and not have the lines she had drawn around him blur even more than they already were?

She could not do this!

CHAPTER THIRTEEN

"MAYBE WE SHOULD go hiking first," Krissy suggested to Jonas.

He gave her a puzzled look. "The store is right there."

She snapped her fingers. "I have an idea. You go in and pick out the ring, and I'll take Chance for a walk. Then you can lock the vehicle."

"I'm not sure why you're so worried about that. It doesn't exactly look like a hotbed of criminal activity," Jonas said, looking up and down the sleepy main street.

She acted as if it was decided. "And then, after you've picked the ring, I'll go in and get it sized."

There. That seemed like a safe way of getting out of a totally awkward situation.

"He'll be fine for a few minutes in the vehicle with the windows down." Was Jonas deliberately missing the point of Krissy's reluctance?

She made one last desperate effort. "Some-one could steal Chance!"

He looked back at Chance and made a face. "Now that seems highly unlikely. Come on. Half the fun is going to be seeing what you pick."

Fun, Krissy reminded herself sternly. She got out of the vehicle, took a deep breath and went around to where Jonas waited by the door. *Sanderson* was etched into the glass. A bell jangled as he opened it and held it for her.

She hesitated, her reluctance to do this deepening. Jonas put his hand on the small of her back and gave her a firm push.

It took a second for her eyes to adjust to the light. They were the only customers. In fact, they were the only people. The store ap-peared to be unmanned.

"I told you it wasn't a hotbed of criminal activity," Jonas said quietly. He took her hand and tugged. "Come on, why don't we start over here?"

She let him guide her over to the display case. The rings glittered up at her. She felt as if she couldn't breathe. She recoiled when she caught sight of the price on one.

"That seems a little much for a ruse," she said, shocked.

"Just play along. Show me the ring you would get if money was no object."

She glanced at him. Could he not see they were messing with a moment most women spent a good deal of their lives dreaming of? Could he not see that after last night this felt like the worst kind of lie?

Not that Krissy had ever indulged such fantasies, but now that she was here, it was hard to ignore the longing. The wish that it was all different.

The wish that she had entered this store with a man that she loved. That they were looking for a ring that symbolized their commitment to each other, a ring that shone with their hopes and dreams for the future.

Jonas was the kind of man who inspired exactly that kind of fantasy.

"What's wrong?" he asked her softly. "Don't be so serious. You're going to get a permanent line, right here."

And then he gently touched her brow with the knuckle of his hand, and she could feel the line of tension evaporate under his touch.

Of course, he was right. She didn't need to be so serious. She could have fun! She could! She pointed at a ring with a huge solitaire diamond. The tag said it was one karat. And that it was worth ten thousand dollars.

"How about that one?"

She had hoped he would reward her choice with shock, and that they would both have a good laugh to break some tension she still held, despite him erasing it from her brow. But Jonas tilted his head and regarded the ring as if it was a serious contender.

"I don't think you could lift up your hand with that thing on it," he said. "How about this one?"

She gazed at the one he was pointing at. It was a smaller diamond, flanked by two emeralds. The price made her gulp.

"It's too much money."

"We weren't going to think about money. Yet. It's just preliminary, to see what you like."

She peered at the display cases. It was making her head ache. There were too many rings, and they represented too many things, and she was pretty sure the frown line was burrowing in deep between her eyes again.

Get it over with, Krissy ordered herself. "How about this one?"

"You're picking it because it's cheaper."

"It's good enough."

"Why do I think the ring out of a candied popcorn box would be good enough for you?"

"Because it would be. It's a game," she reminded him tersely. "You could buy this less expensive one and donate the rest of your budget to a holiday for veterans."

"You really aren't getting into the spirit of this," he chided her. "Most women like shopping for jewelry."

"And you are an expert on that, why?"

He didn't need to answer. She could see it in his face. This was not his first shopping excursion in a jewelry store with a woman.

And probably not his first one the morning after, either. What on earth was she doing?

As the tension snapped in the air between them, a little old man came out from the back. He looked surprised to see customers. He was wearing a jeweler's loupe on a chain around his neck. "My hearing isn't what it used to be. Didn't hear the door." He sized them up, smiled. "Sam Sanderson. How can I help?"

"We were just leaving."

"We're looking for an engagement ring," Jonas said, firmly.

"Inexpensive," she said.

"Ignore her," Jonas said.

Sam's eyes went back and forth between them. Krissy was pretty sure he was thinking *This will never work.*

"My favorite thing," Sam declared happily. "I can feel the hopes and dreams in the air."

She felt a shiver go up and down her spine. Wasn't that exactly the thought she just had about what an engagement ring shopping excursion should be?

"It reminds me of when my Sally and I found the perfect ring," Sam said.

Krissy had the terribly uncomfortable sensation of treading on something sacred.

"She's gone now," Sam continued, "but she still helps sometimes. But you have your own helper already, don't you?"

"Sorry?" Krissy said. It was so much like something that her aunt Jane would have said that she didn't even feel shocked when the man appeared to be nodding at someone over her shoulder.

Jonas, though, turned around, frowning, to look.

"Anything catching your eye here?" the man asked.

"Something inexpensive," Krissy said again, at the same time Jonas, turning back to them, said, "Price is no object."

The man looked back and forth between them again. A smile tickled his lips. He moved to a different case and came back with a small navy-blue velvet box.

He pushed it slowly across the countertop to Krissy.

She hesitated, feeling as if she was part of a spell. Jonas was the one who reached past her and opened the box. The lid creaked open.

Both of them stared at the ring.

"Wow," Jonas said. The truth was he had spent quite a bit of time—and money—in jewelry stores.

It was just the easiest way to say *I had a great evening* or *Here's a little something to remember us by.*

He realized now he was the go-to of a guy who had unabashedly defaulted to superficial in his love life. He was career focused and commitment phobic, and he made no bones about either. Basically, everyone knew the rules going in.

He followed a pretty predictable pattern. There were going to be a few really nice dinners, classic wining and dining, maybe a Broadway show, or a beach or ski weekend trip. The relationship—if it could be called that—was going to be casual, a few good times, some easy laughs. And then it was *adios, señorita.*

A certain kind of woman went for what he offered. Krissy's aunt had gotten it in one glance at him. *Bimbos.*

That seemed a little harsh to him. Still,

buying a bauble for a that kind of woman, even an expensive bauble—or maybe especially an expensive one—soothed something in him and satisfied something in her.

Unfortunately, standing in this little store with Krissy put the whole thing in a different light, and made it seem he had engaged in a series of tawdry business transactions. It all seemed embarrassingly superficial.

So here was the irony: this relationship with Krissy had been 100 percent fake from the outset. And yet everything about it—from getting to know her dog, to eating ice cream treats, to picnicking in the park felt real.

Last night had been one of the most real experiences of Jonas's entire existence, though in all honesty, last night was quickly crowding out memories of his past existence!

But here was the truth: there was an authenticity about Krissy that was shining right through the lie he had convinced her to participate in.

Buying this ring was proving no different.

It was supposed to be part of the game, but it didn't feel like it. Jonas felt invested. He wanted this gift to mean something. He wanted Krissy to love what they bought and remember this time they'd had together forever.

Forever? There was a word Jonas Boyden

avoided. Obviously, it had been a bit of a slip asking her to the opening of his newest resort at the end of summer. This was a one-off.

Still, as he had watched her face as she looked at the jewelry, it was more than obvious that Krissy was not a jewelry person and never had been. She hated this exercise.

And yet the ring she was looking at now had transformed her features. It was an exquisite ring.

It was so *her* in the same way that little black dress had been so her. Classic. Timeless. Understated. Beautiful. The engagement ring was simplicity itself, a circle of perfect diamonds, all the same size, with no central stone.

"There's no price on it," she said hoarsely.

"Good," Jonas said. He lifted the ring from its velvet cushion. As he held it up, it sparked, the diamonds capturing the light and then shooting out blue flames.

Too late, he got how wrong this was, particularly in light of the intimacy they had shared last night. It was taking the whole thing a little too far, but of course, that was something he was known for. He could spend months setting up an elaborate prank.

But as he held out his hand, he was aware this did not feel like part of a prank. He could not take his eyes off her face, the light in it. Krissy caught her tongue between her teeth—that was cute—and then as if caught in the spell, she placed her hand, palm down in his. Her hand felt feminine and soft, and yet there was strength in it, too.

He took a deep breath.

He tried, a little desperately, to remind himself it was a game.

But when he slipped the ring on her engagement finger it felt as if the entire world—and his heart—stood entirely still.

The ring went on easily. It settled at the base of her finger, snug, but not tight. It felt as if it would never come off. It also felt as if it was radiating a strange warmth. Krissy stared at it. He stared at it.

It fit her absolutely perfectly.

"It looks as if it belongs on my hand," she said, stunned. "I've never even worn a ring before."

She looked up at him, something tremulous in her gaze. *Trusting him* to somehow turn this debacle he had started into something with redeeming value.

Jonas realized, stunned, they could see where this was going to take them. It didn't have to be a one-off.

"That's the one," Sam said, not with any question in it at all.

She nodded. Jonas nodded.

She slipped her hand from his. He was aware of not wanting to let it go. Krissy never even took the ring off her finger as the old man rang it up. Sam put the empty box in a little silk bag and handed it to her.

"When's the wedding?" he asked.

"The long weekend," Jonas said.

"That soon! But what about the wedding band?"

Jonas did not often find himself in situations where he was not in control, where he was caught off-balance, but this seemed to be spinning out of his control. Sam fetched the matching band for the ring and showed it to them.

Jonas found himself nodding that they'd take that, too, and the ring was put it in a box and handed to him.

Sam wagged a stern finger at him. "Don't put that on her finger until you've said your vows. It's bad luck. If it doesn't fit properly, bring it back then."

Jonas found himself nodding like an obedient schoolboy. He needed to remind himself that second ring was never going on her finger.

Unless they decided to see where this would take them. He could feel his heart beating unreasonably.

"Have you got your license? You should run over to the town hall and get it here. It's just on the corner over there. There's never a lineup. One more thing off the list."

"I'm sure they're not open Saturdays," Jonas said uncomfortably.

"Yup! Yup, they are. Closed Sundays and Mondays."

Krissy shot him a look that said they weren't going to get a license! They stepped out of the store and checked on Chance. He was snoring in the back seat.

Jonas rocked back on his heels and looked down the street.

It had all become a bit too serious for him. Even his own thoughts were veering into deep into uncharted territory. He needed to get this back to a light place, a place where he was comfortable, where they both were aware it was just a game they were playing. It was supposed to be fun!

Then a plan hatching—and maybe feeling a little pressured by Sam, who was watching expectantly from the window—he took her hand and headed for the town hall.

"We are not going to the town hall," Krissy

told Jonas firmly, trying to extricate her hand. "That's taking it all too far. It's going to be awful enough when you return the rings."

"I'm not returning the rings."

"Of course you are! What use would you have for a ring like this? And the wedding band?"

"None whatsoever. You can keep it."

"Wh-what?"

"I get the car. There should be something in it for you."

"I'm not keeping a ring from a phony engagement," she said. "And I certainly don't want a fake wedding band."

"The band itself is not fake," he pointed out.

"I deduced that from the price."

"You can have them made into something else, then," he said, dismissing it.

"We are absolutely not going to the town hall!"

CHAPTER FOURTEEN

SUDDENLY IT FELT imperative to Jonas to get Krissy into that town hall to apply for a marriage license.

Not to make it more real, but to make it less so, an essential piece of an elaborate—but fun—stunt.

"Why not?" he said persuasively. "It's just a piece of paper. It's a marriage license, not a marriage. Just think if I can show Theresa and Mike a marriage license. It's the coup de grâce!"

"Coup de grâce is actually a French term that translates to killing blow."

Who knew things like that? She did. This wonderfully complex, smart, sweet, sexy woman, who was wearing his ring. On her engagement finger.

He had to keep the scam part of this exercise in the forefront. But hadn't it moved out of that territory last night? Hadn't he just been thinking they could take it beyond the weekend reunion—after he'd won the bet— and see where it went?

He was never confused! He was not going to let confusion rule now, not this late in his life.

He was keeping his eye on the prize! But his eyes moved to her.

His hand in hers was a mistake. He loved touching her casually like this, as if it was the most natural thing in the world.

Come to that, it felt like the most natural thing in the world.

How was that possible? He was on the town hall steps, about to fill out paperwork for a life commitment, and it felt natural. And good.

He let go of her hand as if it had burned him. He thrust his own offending hand deep into his pocket.

"You're right," he said, coming to his senses. "This is taking it too far, even for me, master of the elaborate prank."

He felt an uneasy awareness that the prize did not feel like his car, no matter how hard he tried to make that the focus.

The prize felt like her.

Krissy frowned at Jonas's sudden uncertainty. It seemed very unlike him. For the first time since she had met him, he seemed a little off. Uneasy. Distracted. No doubt the cost of that excursion in the jewelry store had caught him a bit by surprise.

"No," she said firmly, "Let's go get the license. You're right—it's just a piece of paper. And if it will help convince your family, it's a good return on your investment in this."

She held up the ring. It caught the light and winked at her and made her heart do a delicious flip-flop.

Silly as it was, she felt totally different since he'd put that ring on her finger. Not just connected to Jonas, but alive. Bold. Aware of life sizzling with the potential for surprises, for delight, for amazement.

At the best of times, life was all just a game, wasn't it? Why not just enjoy it?

"I'm prepared to earn the ring," she told him decisively. "How much was it, again? The whole *'Now you need a wedding band'* thing distracted me."

He didn't say anything, still looking warily up the steps.

"I'll start earning it right now," she decided. "I will play the part of your absolutely besotted betrothed. I'll reprise my queen role."

"You sucked at being the queen."

She pretended offense. "I could tone it down a notch. Princess."

"Would I have to be a prince?"

"Let's not get carried away. A frog will do."

She was relieved when he smiled and shrugged his shoulders as if he was rolling out from under a big weight.

He did a surprisingly good impression of a frog, and when she laughed, he did it again. And then they were both laughing, and that strange tension she had seen in him was gone.

"You have to stop being a frog now, or I won't be able to keep a straight face while we do the paperwork. I would imagine a straight face is required."

They went up the steps, and he opened the front door of the town hall for her. He leaned in close to her ear.

"Ribbit," he croaked.

"Stop it!"

"There's only one way to turn a frog into a prince," he reminded her.

"Never mind being a prince." She did not want to think about kissing him. "You can be a knight to my princess."

"As long as you don't expect shining armor," he told her.

"Tarnished will do."

He grinned. He opened the door to the

inner office for her. "Milady," he murmured as she went through.

He seemed to Krissy's great relief to be back to his normal self. They found themselves standing in a dusty and poorly lit town office. The laughter must have still been shining between them, because the clerk, her gray hair in tight curls, looked faintly disapproving as she slapped the paperwork down in front of them and checked their identification.

She was immune to Jonas's rather substantial charm.

"You can't use it for twenty-four hours," the clerk told them sternly. "And you have to use it within sixty days or it's void."

See? Jonas mouthed to Krissy, *Void.*

"It's forty dollars," the clerk told them, as if that was a great deal of money, and they should have thought more carefully before spending it, "but that includes the issuance of the certificate of marriage. The officiant—the person who performs your ceremony—can send it to me—the address is here—and then the record of your marriage will be on file."

"That may have been the best forty dollars I ever spent," Jonas said, standing at the top of the town hall steps.

They both stared at the document for a

moment before he folded it and put it in his pocket.

"What do you think? Something to eat and a hike?"

Marriage license, check. Time to think of food. Such a man thing! So delightful!

She thought, if she was sensible, she should just go home.

But somehow it seemed a little late to be applying good sense to this situation. Besides, Jonas was taking the whole thing lightly, treating it like a lark. He had regained his equilibrium; in fact, he was practically clicking his heels as they left the town hall.

Why be the stick-in-the-mud? Why let on that there was something terribly unsettling about playing with these sacred institutions? Something terribly unsettling about the fact they had shared such powerful intimacies, already, and no doubt would again, before this was over.

Over.

In a little more than a week—after next weekend—the game would be over. She'd probably never see him again. No sense paying any attention to the downward swish in her stomach at that thought. Wasn't there at least a chance that it didn't have to end?

Last night had been incredible. If Jonas

didn't like where it was going, wouldn't he have hightailed it and run today?

No, he had made a choice to ignore the *complications*. It could even be argued he had complicated things further by buying those rings.

The marriage license, their names joined together on a single piece of paper, complicated things even more. Though they had thought they could escape the implications of such a solemn piece of paper, the very process of applying for it, the fact it was nestled in his pocket, created connection between them.

Obviously, they had incredible chemistry. Obviously, they shared a sense of humor. Obviously, they had fun together. Plus, they both loved the dog!

Was there going to be an awful price for accepting the invitation in his laughing eyes? To let go? To have fun? To embrace the joy life offered?

Krissy faced an awful truth. There was a terrible chance of falling in love with her fake fiancé. She was pretty sure she was halfway there already.

And as powerless to stop it as she had ever been over anything in her entire life.

She surrendered to it.

He did, too.

The rest of the day, they acted as if there were no complications between them at all.

They acted as if they were exactly what they were: fresh young lovers in the throes of discovery. They ate crunchy croissants at a dog-friendly patio outside a bakery not far from the town hall.

When they got back in the vehicle, an ecstatic Chance was somehow on her lap instead of in the back. His huge head was out the window, his tongue lolling happily as they drove through the beautiful countryside, the spring air flowing through her window—the utter happiness of these moments—felt like she was breathing in wine.

Jonas parked in the lot at the head of the trail that he had obviously hiked many times. They held hands as they hiked a winding trail that went up a mountain. He was not dressed for hiking, and his shoes were terrible for it.

The trail was steep and challenging in places. Jonas pulled her over slippery rocks and piggybacked her across a rushing creek, probably wrecking the shoes completely. The trail ended at a waterfall and a turquoise pool. The water was frigid, but they splashed each other, took off their shoes and chased barefoot through the mud. They threw sticks for

Chance, who would bring them back and shake all over them.

Between Chance and the mist from the falls, they were soon soaked, their clothes clinging to them, a reminder of how things had gotten out of hand last night.

But it didn't feel out of hand as their lips met. It felt as if life had conspired to give them each other. In the rainbow hues of its mist, they kissed until they were breathless with it.

Jonas picked the tiny yellow wildflowers that grew in abundance on the banks of the pool, and he decorated the dog's collar and then he threaded them through her hair. And then she picked wildflowers and added them to the dog's collar and threaded them through Jonas's hair.

They laughed until she felt as if she couldn't breathe.

They'd stopped for dinner at a little roadside hot dog stand, that Jonas claimed had the best hot dogs ever. He still had a flower in his hair, and she didn't tell him.

The stand featured more varieties of hot dogs than Krissy had known existed. She ordered a chili dog, Jonas ordered the hot dog version of a Triple Chocolate Volcano Sunday. Chance had two plain dogs, no bun.

Halfway through she traded hot dogs with Jonas.

Funny how wonderful it felt, just one of those little intimacies that couples shared. They lingered over refills of sodas until the sun went down, laughing, chatting, teasing.

Krissy never wanted this day to end. And then it didn't.

Because when they got back to her house, Jonas walked her to the door and leaned into her.

She thought he was going to kiss her. Again. She ached for the taste of his lips. Even though they had been kissing all day, she felt she could not get enough.

His lips had become her drug.

But it was even better than a good-night kiss.

His voice raw with need, he said, "Can I come in, Krissy?"

Jonas woke up the next morning to his feet asleep under the weight of the dog, and Krissy nestled into his arm.

He was aware of the sound of rain hammering the roof of her little cottage, and contentment unfolded in him like a cat getting up from in front of the fire to stretch.

He slipped out of bed before her, found her washing machine and tossed his clothes in. With a towel tucked around his waist, he made coffee and brought it to her.

She blinked at his towel. "Is that what you're wearing today?"

"I certainly hope not," he said, and let the towel slip.

After that, they drank coffee gone cold, and they shared a real newspaper in her bed. Jonas usually read his on his tablet, so reading the paper like this felt old-fashioned and delightful. But as they read snippets of articles to each other, he wondered what didn't feel delightful with her.

They had cereal for breakfast and put his clothes in the dryer. She walloped him at Scrabble. They finally got dressed. They squeezed under one umbrella and took the dog for a walk. Being wet again had the same predictable effect on them.

They showered the chill away; they ate macaroni and cheese for lunch and then baked cookies and ate them in bed, warm chocolate from melted chips dripping down their lips and inviting the most delightful cleanup.

Jonas was a man whose life had taken him in many unexpected directions and given him many surprising adventures. The nature of his work led him to experiences most people would never have, perfect tens on the scale of excitement.

He had traveled the globe, to some of the most exotic places in the world.

He had helicopter skied in the Rocky Mountains and been on beaches in Saint-Tropez. He had zip-lined and been on a photo safari.

He had been a guest at castles and estates and ranches.

He had hobnobbed with royalty and some of the world's most celebrated stars and athletes, been to their galas and games and award shows.

And all of that—every single bit of it—paled in comparison to a rainy afternoon, with the dog smelling damp and Krissy in her robe, sprawled across the bed reading him the funnies from the Sunday morning paper and sharing a chocolate chip cookie with him.

CHAPTER FIFTEEN

"WHAT THE HECK is that?"

It was Monday morning, and Krissy was in the school staff room. It was the last week of school and there was a certain giddiness in the air.

And a giddiness inside of her, unlike anything she had ever felt. Jonas had left late yesterday afternoon.

And so far, she had received half a dozen texts from him and a video of him doing an impression of Kermit and making frog sounds. In the video, which Krissy had watched more times than she could count, she caught glimpses of the sumptuous apartment he lived in.

Fellow teacher Artie Calhoun grabbed her hand and hooted. "Engaged! Look guys, Krissy is engaged!"

Shocked, she realized she had not taken off her ring. Shocked, she realized the ring already felt like part of her. She had not even considered removing it this morning. But now she was swarmed by her fellow teachers, congratulating her, asking questions, excited for her.

"I didn't even know you had a boyfriend!" Martha Montrose crowed. "Who is it? What's his name?"

Krissy wasn't sure of the wisdom of making any of this public. It would have been such a simple thing to take off that ring! In September she'd come back to school. She'd still own the ring, but would she still wear it? Explanations would be needed.

On the other hand, was it possible she and Jonas would still be going out as summer wound down?

After the weekend together it seemed impossible that they wouldn't be! It felt as if her life could no longer be complete without him, and from the nature of his texts, he was feeling the very same way.

"Jonas," she said. "Jonas Boyden."

Martha's phone came out of her purse, and she plucked at it furiously. She squealed. "Krissy, he's gorgeous! Look at this," she called to the other staff members. "Krissy's guy is a multimillionaire. He owns a company called Last Resort. Good grief, he is part owner of Yummy Mommy."

Thankfully, the bell rang, and Krissy was able to get away from the awed well-wishers all around her.

Excitement was high in the classroom, and she found herself relaxing into it, instead of trying to control it. She giggled with the kids. She played games with them. They sang songs together.

At the end of the day, Georgie came and regarded her thoughtfully. "You're so happy," he declared.

After he and the other children had gone, she contemplated that her happiness was so obvious that even a child could see it.

And what did that mean about the way she had been before? She hadn't felt unhappy.

But she hadn't felt like this, either.

Caring about someone just made everything better! The flowers looked brighter, and the air smelled fresher, and the world seemed funnier and friendlier. The week passed in a flurry of texts and phone calls between her and Jonas, but both their schedules precluded meeting. The last week of school was always crammed with activities and responsibilities. Normally, after that final Friday afternoon of tears and hugs and kisses from all her kindergarten students, Krissy would go home and feel bereft for days, summer looming large and empty.

But this year, all she felt was excited. Jonas was coming tonight, and tomorrow they were going to his reunion. She was meeting his family.

It was crazy to be so excited.

It was crazy for her heart to beat so hard every time the phone rang, every time a text pinged.

When she opened the door to him that night and looked into Jonas's face, saw the hunger in his eyes and the tender smile on his lips, the truth hit her.

The truth was Krissy was crazy in love.

With her fake fiancé.

But when he reached for her, when he pulled her into him, when his lips claimed hers and lit that now-familiar fire within her, it was the most real thing Krissy had ever felt.

The weather was glorious the next day as they made an early start to the Catskills, but the feeling inside of her put the sun to shame.

She loved his family resort from her first glance of the log arch over the road. A sign swung from it: Boy's Den. Underneath that hung a smaller sign that promised Dog-Gone Fun. Because Jonas had told her the story of the rebirth of the resort, when Krissy recognized the motto she already felt connected to it in some way.

"I told my sister to change the name from Boy's Den, but she wouldn't. My dad named it, and he thought it was such a clever play on the family name. None of us had the heart to tell him it was a terrible name, that it sounded like a Boy Scout camp or worse, a den of ill repute."

"I love it," Krissy said firmly, and what's more, she already loved his sister for keeping it.

They drove down a curving driveway, shaded on both sides by enormous sugar maples, into a clearing where a small river crashed over rocks into a large body of water that was not quite a lake, but too big to be a pond. There was a sandy beach and a raft bobbed up and down out on the water. Though it was before lunch, the day promised to be hot, and there was already a group of teenagers on the raft, boys showing off for girls by pitching each other in the water.

"How many people come to your family reunion?" Krissy asked. There were people everywhere.

"It varies. More than a hundred. Less than two."

"A hundred people in a family?"

He laughed. "That's how many come. My dad was from a huge family—six brothers and two sisters. My mom was like you, an only child, and I bet she had that same look on her face when she was introduced to this mob."

Jonas stopped the vehicle in front of a rustic log building that must have been the main lodge, and a woman Krissy knew instantly was his sister came off a large covered veranda to meet them as they got out of the car. Two little boys tumbled down the steps behind her, and Jonas swept one up in each arm.

"Simon. Gar!" His arms full of children, he leaned over and kissed his sister on the cheek.

The boys squealed their delight, insisted their names were Harry and Danny, but Jonas acted baffled and told them they were mistaken, and that he had a long-standing relationship with Simon and Gar and knew who they were. He bantered with them until the laughter of the boys filled the air.

Krissy could not take her eyes off the three of them, a light of love and joy shining from them. She was totally aware this was the kind of daddy Jonas would be. Strong, engaged, fun-filled. It filled her with the most exquisite tenderness she had ever felt.

She was aware of his sister watching her. "He's great with kids," she offered. "Do you think you'll be having any?"

"Hey!" Jonas said, giving his sister a warning look and putting down the boys. "You haven't even been introduced yet."

Danny and Harry switched their rambunctious affection to the dog, who was thrilled.

Jonas introduced them and Theresa greeted Krissy as if she had known her all her life. She was warm and unpretentious, and Krissy's feeling of loving his sister was already deepened.

"Now how did Jonas keep you secret?" she asked, folding Krissy into a firm hug. "Oh, look at that ring! Mike and I thought he was toying with us when he called and told us he was engaged, but he's not, is he?"

Thankfully, before Krissy answered, the boys started fighting over who the dog liked best, and Theresa calmly pulled them apart.

"And look at you!" Theresa said. She got down in front of Chance and took his face in her hands, kissed him right on his ugly snout. "I can tell he's got a great soul."

Krissy's feeling of homecoming intensified.

"Do you want a tour of the place?" she asked when she got back up. "Jonas, take the boys and find Mike. He's building a mud pit. We thought we'd add a tug-of-war to the water fight this year."

"Do you think we could unpack first before you put me to work?" Jonas groused, but shrugged ruefully at Krissy, called his nephews, and they headed off. "Do not interrogate her," he warned his sister.

Chance looked momentarily torn before giving Krissy a guilty look and taking off after Jonas and the boys.

Theresa laughed. "Dogs always love him. Of course I'm going to interrogate you," she said. "I want to know everything about the woman my brother has fallen for."

But as it turned out, the interrogation, thankfully, had to wait. The resort was a cluster of about a dozen adorable weathered gray log cabins. They were on a slight hill behind the lodge and were in a wide horseshoe that faced the lake. The cabins were also called dens, each named after a wild animal. Bear, Rabbit, Deer, Beaver, Skunk and so on.

"Believe it or not, Skunk Den is our most requested cabin. My dad named them," Theresa said with rueful affection. All seemed to be occupied by members of the Boyden clan. There was also a growing tent city on the edge of the lake. They could not walk two steps without Theresa being stopped, greetings exchanged, questions asked, introductions made.

There were cousins, aunts, uncles, great-aunts, great-uncles, until Krissy's head was spinning with names.

Every time she was introduced as Jonas's fiancée, instead of feeling guilty about the lie, it seemed to become more real. She was embraced and kissed and congratulated and welcomed completely into the ranks as if she'd been born to this large, loud, happy clan.

The sound of happiness was in the air: children laughing, the low hum of conversation, the call of a name, an occasional shout, splashing and shrieking at the beach. Dogs barked and birds sang.

It was family as Krissy, as a child, had longed for, family like she had read about in books and seen in movies.

"There are so many people," Krissy said.

"We always have the family reunion first before we open for the year," Theresa told her. "It could be a very lucrative weekend, but its family first for us."

Family first, Krissy repeated inwardly, and something sighed within her. Perfect contentment.

Jonas watched Krissy. This was his moment: mission accomplished. She was currently on the opposite team of the tug-of-war. She was pulling with all her might, but still his team was inching them toward the mud bog in the middle.

Children were shrieking and dogs were barking, but it felt as if his whole world suddenly went silent, his focus sharp around her.

Her head was thrown back with laughter. Her every muscle was braced. Her hair was free and tumbling around her face, her nose sunburned.

His team made their move, a sudden jerk and the other team was flying toward them, then stumbling over each other, and then falling in a tangle of limbs and shouted laughter into the mud.

Krissy was screaming with laughter. She pulled herself up—her clothes absolutely plastered to her—grabbed mud balls in both fists and came after him. He ran, and she ran after him, pelting him with the mud. He turned on her, scooped her up in his arms. She twisted and tried to free herself, but to the cheers of his family, he stomped into the middle of the mud bog and released her.

Except she didn't let go. She wrapped her arms tight around his neck, and he lost his footing in the greasy muck, and they went down in the slop together. His nephews led the charge of children who were suddenly all around him, squishing mud into his hair and down his shirt.

"Enough," he finally roared, rising to his

feet and shaking children off him like a dog shaking off water. He held out his hand to her and she took it, and to the wild cheers of his family, he pulled her hard against himself and kissed her muddy lips. And then he scooped her up again, and with the children racing after them shouting encouragement, he ran into the lake and tossed her and then dived in behind her.

She emerged clean and dripping and he stared at her.

"My weakness," he said in a voice only she could hear, "seeing you wet."

The water had been freezing, but the sudden heat in her eyes warmed him through to his core.

He didn't care who was watching. He scooped her up again and took her to the cabin they would share.

Later that night, they sat at the campfire, sparks shooting up into an inky dark sky. Krissy's mouth was smeared with melted marshmallow and chocolate from the s'mores she had taken from his fingertips. Jonas decided he'd better not look at her lips anymore.

Chance was nestled between his nephews on the other side of the fire. All three of them were utterly exhausted.

The guitars came out, an accordion, a tambourine, a harmonica. His brother-in-law, Mike, had a good voice, and he led the sing-along.

The sing-along was a disaster as always: people sometimes knew the chorus, but not the words. His uncle Fred had too many beers and was singing too loudly and totally out of tune. The kids were getting tired and querulous.

Including his nephews, who began a fistfight over which one of them Chance loved best.

Jonas got up from beside Krissy and picked up Danny. His sister was right beside him and picked up Harry. Both boys were asleep on their shoulders before they reached the lodge.

He tucked Danny into his pint-size racing car bed, and his sister did the same with Harry. She disappeared for a minute and came back with a facecloth, which she handed to Jonas. He brushed the worst of the s'more remains from Danny's face.

"You're going to be a good dad, Jonas. And she's going to be a good mom. I love the two of you together."

He realized, not once had either his sister or his brother-in-law mentioned the bet or the stupid car. They were just genuinely happy for him.

And when he looked inside himself, he didn't find a lie.

He found genuine happiness, too.

"When are you going to get married?" Theresa asked him. "If this afternoon was any indication, you should make it soon."

"This afternoon?"

She rolled her eyes. "Disappearing into the cabin for an hour."

"Oh, yeah, this afternoon," he said. He was blushing. You didn't talk about stuff like that with your sister. "We have the license," he heard himself saying, as if he had to excuse his afternoon excursion to her.

"You do?"

"Yeah. We'll just, ah, slip away one weekend and quietly tie the knot. You know, just the two of us."

He wasn't prepared for the look of devastation on his sister's face.

"You mean without family? Without me?"

He realized he should tell her the truth, right now, right this minute. But he could hear laughter drifting up from the campfire. And Jonas was suddenly aware he wasn't quite sure what the truth was.

He heard a loud popping sounds.

"Somebody is setting off fireworks," she said. "I hope it doesn't wake the boys."

"It won't."

They walked back out of the lodge. Down

at the edge of the lake, the fireworks were starting. He found Krissy. Someone had given her a blanket, and she opened it up, inviting him to sit on the bench beside her.

A firework exploded in the sky above them, and she leaned into him.

"This one's called Bite Your Tushy," he told her.

"Fireworks have names?" she said skeptically.

"They do."

"You're making that up."

"Nope. And this one is called Chasing Booty."

"Are you serious?"

As the fireworks went off, he named them for her—One Bad Mother, Hot Dog, Loyal to None—loving her giggle at the crazy, slightly off-color names, her sighs of awe as the night sky lit up and reflected in the lake.

It seemed there was so much that he wanted her to know, so much that he wanted to show her, so much that she knew and that she could show him.

A lifetime wouldn't be nearly long enough, he thought, and his lips found the top of her head and kissed it.

CHAPTER SIXTEEN

"WHAT'S GOING ON down there?" Krissy asked Jonas the next morning. They were sitting out on the small deck of their cabin, sipping coffee, the dog at their feet. Krissy was not sure she had ever felt like this: such a sense of belonging, of happiness, a pure contentment.

The perfection of the morning was marred only by the staccato pounding of a hammer.

"My uncle Fred is a minister. He holds a church service the Sunday of the reunion. He appears to be building something."

"Are we going?" she asked. "To the church service?"

"Huh? Why wouldn't we? Everybody goes."

"I've never been a churchgoer, but I'm pretty sure the devout would regard what has been going on between us as a sin."

"You know the guy leading 'Ninety-Nine Bottles of Beer on the Wall' last night? After having consumed at least that many? That's Uncle Fred."

"And he's a minister?"

"Yeah. So you know what they say about stones. Not that what has been going on between us feels anything like a sin." He smiled at her with bone-melting wickedness. "Feels more like heaven to me."

"Fred, the leader of drinking songs, is also a minister?"

"Welcome to that crazy, convoluted thing called family."

She laughed, but then grew serious. If what had been going on between them didn't feel like a sin—and it certainly didn't—something else did.

"That's how I feel, Jonas. I feel welcomed to your family. I don't know how we're going to tell them it has all been a charade."

"Has it felt like a charade to you, Krissy?" he asked quietly.

"No," she said. "It hasn't."

"Not to me, either," he said, his voice a low growl that tickled along her spine like his touch. "I think we should see where this could go."

She stared at him. She could feel tears pricking her eyes. "Me, too," she whispered.

He reached out and put the back of his

hand against her cheek. He leaned into her, but something below them crashed, and was followed by some pretty liberal cussing.

"Is that your uncle Fred?"

"None other," he said drily. "What the heck are they doing down there? They're building something. That's strange. What would they need to build for a service?"

Krissy got up with her coffee and stood at the deck railing. She craned her neck. "It's an arbor," she said.

"Really? That's—

"Good morning, lovebirds."

It was Theresa coming up the steps to their cabin. "Jonas, I've had the best idea!"

"Oh-oh," he said, raising an eyebrow at his sister. "Why are you making me nervous?"

"I couldn't even sleep last night, thinking about what you told me. That you and Krissy are just going to go and get married by yourselves somewhere. It doesn't make sense. It's something we all want to celebrate with you. Why not do it here?"

Krissy sneaked a look at Jonas.

He looked utterly gobsmacked. His eyes met hers. He looked away. They had agreed they were going to see where this was going, but he was not prepared for this. How could he be?

"Krissy, what do you think?" Theresa

asked. She was so excited. "He'd never forget your anniversary. It would fall on the reunion weekend and his birthday!"

"You mean have a wedding?" Krissy asked, not sure she could be hearing right. "At next year's reunion?"

"No! Right now!"

Krissy's heart was nearly pounding out of her chest. She dared not even look at Jonas, afraid her heart would be broken in two by his reaction to his sister's crazy suggestion.

"Look, I know you mean well, Theresa, but Krissy doesn't even have a dress. You don't just get married in your shorts. Do you?"

Krissy shot him a look. All the things he could have said, and he was worried she didn't have a dress?

"I have a dress," Theresa whispered.

"Nobody has an extra wedding dress just lying around," Jonas said. "Look, you're ambushing us, and—"

"Ambushing you? You said you were going to do it anyway. You said you had the license. I bet you even have a wedding band, don't you? I mean, probably not with you, but—"

"I have it with me," he said.

Krissy felt her eyes go wide. He did?

"I haven't taken it out of my pocket since I bought it," he confessed, his voice low.

There was something in his voice—uncertain and pained—that Krissy heard. He'd been carrying that ring around with him?

She looked at his face. He was looking at her. He had the look on his face that she had seen ever since the first time they had made love.

It was the look of a man who couldn't believe his luck. It was a look that was protective and tender and awed. It was the look of a man who had been swept away by an unexpected current in his life.

By a river.

And the river was called Love.

She knew it, suddenly, to the bottom of her bones. Jonas loved her. And she loved him. There were people who would say that they hadn't known each other long enough, that they could not know if it was love after such a short period of time. There would be people who would say it was an infatuation. Chemistry.

But there was a place in her soul that *knew*. She knew deeply and completely. She might have known from the moment she laid eyes on him outside the front door of Match Made in Heaven.

She belonged with this man. He belonged with her. To her.

This was what her aunt had believed. This was what her aunt had always tried to tell her. That love was a cosmic force, powerful and immutable. That there were people who were made for each other, and Aunt Jane had believed it was her calling in life to find those people and bring them together.

Had this been her aunt's final match? What if even death could not stop her aunt from doing what she felt was her sacred duty?

"What do you think?" Theresa asked, looking back and forth between them.

"What do you think?" Jonas asked Krissy. And she heard the oddest thing in his voice. He was the most confident, self-assured man she had ever met.

And yet there was no mistaking that was fear in his voice. Jonas Boyden, millionaire, self-made man, was afraid that Krissy Clark, a schoolteacher, did not feel the same way as him right now.

"I think that's the best idea I've ever heard," she said.

Jonas let out a whoop. He turned from where he'd been standing at the deck to lift her out of her chair.

But Theresa inserted herself between them. "Uh-uh. After you're married."

"It's just a little late for that," Jonas said

grouchily, gazing over his sister's shoulder at Krissy's lips with such wanting that she shivered from it.

"Come on," Theresa said to Krissy, "we've got lots to do. And you," she said to her brother, "go see Mike. And make sure you have that ring with you."

"Yes, ma'am," Jonas said meekly.

Jonas felt as if he was in a dream. The best dream he had ever had. Somehow, this crazy family of his had, in a matter of hours, put together a wedding.

The arbor that they had been building that morning was now so thickly braided with balsam fir boughs that he could not see the structure underneath it. As the summer sun drenched it, the fragrance enveloped him. Beyond the arbor, the lake where he had grown, where the days of his boyhood had unfolded, winked and sparkled.

Mike was at Jonas's side, and his family was slowly filling up the chairs that had fragrant boughs attached to them with burlap bows. He was aware, as perhaps he never had been before, how this gathering of aunts and uncles and cousins and nephews all held the spark of his parents' blood. His parents were gone, and yet here, too.

For the first time, Jonas understood. What was best about them had gone on. What was best about them demanded he be brave enough to accept this gift that had been given to him. Love.

Their love was here, standing with him, in each of these people gathered, and that love went on and on.

With that realization, everything around Jonas took on a shimmering radiance: birdsong, bees humming, blades of grass, the wrinkles on his aunt Martha's carefully folded hands, the cobalt blue of his uncle Hal's shirt.

His cousin Shandra placed a flute to her lips, and the sound that came from that flute increased Jonas's sense of being on heaven's door. The melody lifted and soared, dipped and fell, rose again.

Harry and Danny came first: in shorts and little plaid shirts, with ties. Harry's tie was already askew, and Danny's cowlick already defied Theresa's efforts to tame it. Chance was sandwiched in between them, burlap pack bags slapping him on either side. The boys were pulling leaves and wild white daisies from the sacks and throwing them in the air and at the assembled with just a little too much enthusiasm. Aunt Vera caught Harry's arm and said something stern to him that subdued his flower tossing.

Jonas smiled at that, and then the smile faltered. His breath died like a breeze would die in the hottest part of the day. Down a shaded path that curved through beech and hemlock and oak, he caught a glimpse of Krissy coming.

She was wearing a short white dress that pinched at her waist and then flared out and flowed over her like water. Her shoulders, sun-kissed, were bare. So, too, were her feet, he noticed. She was wearing a ring of flowers on her head, the snowy white of Queen Anne's lace interwoven with waxy green leaves and the soft lavender of dame's rocket. In that intricately woven ring, he saw the hands of the matriarchs of all these clans weaving her into the family.

Her hair flowed free, untamed, gorgeous, from under that ring of flowers. Her hands were clasped in front of her, and in them was a bouquet of deep blue lupines, his mother's favorite flowers.

Jonas had never seen anything, or anyone, as beautiful as the woman gliding toward him.

Confident.

Not a queen.

And not a warrior.

Not even a princess.

Something better.

A woman who did not have to play any role at all. Who had found herself and had found her way of being in the world. So sure of herself, so genuine, so authentic that it shone from her. She was pure love.

She was a goddess.

Her eyes never left his face.

And in those eyes was every man's deepest dream, a dream he did not even know he had, until it walked toward him with sun kissing delicate curves and joyous tears streaming down a serene face.

Jonas marveled at the glory of a world that could bring him someone like her.

Krissy arrived beside him and they looked at each other. He saw the wonder in her gaze, a look a man could die to receive.

Fred cleared his throat, reminding them they could not get lost in each other and block out all else just yet.

Jonas noted that his happy-go-lucky uncle had somehow transformed into a man of quiet authority.

The age-old ritual of two people joining together in front of the community that would love and support them began.

Jonas, because of his large family, had been to dozens of weddings. And yet never had the words resonated so deeply with him, never had he felt the sacredness of the vows so intensely as when he was saying them. It felt, not as if the words were leaving him, but as if they were entering him, becoming part of his muscle, his cells, his bones, his soul.

For better, for worse.

For richer, for poorer.

In sickness and in health.

To love and to cherish.

Till death do us part.

And then, just when he thought the experience could not intensify anymore, Krissy, so beloved to him in such a short time, was saying those words to him, her voice strong and sure, her gaze steady on his face.

He could feel the promise, weaving together with his promises to her, making something brand-new in the world, strong, invincible.

And then they were declared husband and wife, and to the cheers of the assembled, they kissed each other.

A kiss that said welcome home.

A kiss that promised it would stretch toward eternity.

A kiss that filled every void that neither of them had known they still carried.

After a long, long time, they came up for air. Jonas rose out of the silence of their joined lips like a swimmer coming from the bottom of a body of water, breaking the surface. His family was cheering. His sister was crying. Mike was grinning ear to ear. Chance was moaning. His nephews were pelting the gathering with flowers and leaves.

He took Krissy's hand. It felt so right in his, a perfect fit. He gazed down at her, and she drank him in with wonder. Finally, they turned and walked down the aisle. The gathering had been waiting, and daisy petals floated around them until it felt as if they were walking through a blizzard.

How right his sister had been that this was the kind of moment that was not just about two people.

This moment, this celebration of hope, this confirmation of love, this confidence in the future, was not just for Krissy and Jonas.

It was for all of them.

Love was a gift that radiated outward to the whole world.

CHAPTER SEVENTEEN

KRISSY AWOKE IN the morning, sun pouring through the red and white oaks that shaded their cabin and dappling her face. Her feet hurt, in the best possible way, and a smile tickled her lips as she remembered dancing into the wee hours of the morning.

No doubt that was why she was exhausted, despite having slept soundly.

In her husband's arms.

She realized the place beside her in bed was empty, but she turned to the rumpled sheets and touched them. Buried her nose in his pillow and drank in the scent of him.

She was married to Jonas Boyden.

It was almost too big to comprehend. Ever since they had driven under those gateposts onto the resort, it felt as if enchantment had unfolded.

An enchantment where love was fanned to life, where every moment shone brilliantly, where the impossible became possible, where what was considered *normal* was suspended.

Krissy realized she needed to see Jonas to make sure she was not having a dream. She climbed from the bed, showered, pulled a comb through her hair and tossed on some shorts and a T-shirt.

There was always coffee on the front porch of the main lodge, and she was sure she would find Jonas there.

She heard him before she saw him, among the deep rise and fall of male voices. She stopped, loving that she knew him so well that she could tell which voice was his. She loved the sound of it, the pure masculine vibrancy, and she felt a quiver as she remembered how his voice had worshipped her last night.

Beautiful.

My heart.

My love.

But then he stopped talking. And she heard the other voice. Mike?

"I have to give it to you, buddy, you went the extra mile to keep that car."

Just as she had recognized his voice, now she recognized Jonas's shout of laughter. Everything in Krissy's world felt as if it was crashing down around her. She did not wait to hear his response.

This was what the enchantment had kept her from seeing, had kept her from remembering, had kept her from focusing on.

From the beginning, it had been a deception.

Her eagerness not to be alone on a weekend that would have intensified her sense of having lost her family and best friend, her aunt Jane, had clouded out reason, had clouded out fact, had clouded out *everything*.

And now that the first doubt had wiggled its way past the shining walls of the enchantment, others crowded in.

What kind of idiot followed through, turning what was supposed to be a game into reality? What kind of fool got married on an impulse?

Sickly, Krissy realized exactly who got married on an impulse.

Her parents had. An impulse, and because they had to. Because momentary passion had led to a permanent situation, an unwanted pregnancy.

She suddenly saw her exhaustion this morning in a completely different light. She counted back to the first time she and Jonas had spent the night together. She realized her cycle was off.

She had been so swept up in the magic of

what had been unfolding between her and Jonas that she had forgotten that stark possibility.

She was a science major! How could she, of all people, have forgotten the biology of what a man and a woman together could produce? How could she have been so reckless? She had acted without reason, swept away in a tsunami of passion. She hadn't asked him to take precautions, and he had probably assumed she was on the pill.

But she wasn't. She'd given up on love. She knew better. She'd made the very reasonable decision, based on facts, that love was a whirlpool that sucked in everything around it and tossed the wreckage back out when it was done.

Was she pregnant?

The fear that overtook her made her heart pound.

Because this was her parents all over again. A marriage that should have never been held together by a poor baby, born with a job, a responsibility.

Krissy turned quickly away from the lodge before anybody saw her. She started to run through the trees toward the cabin, panic driving her.

Calm yourself, she said as she arrived back

at the cabin. She had to make rational decisions. And that was never going to happen as long as Jonas was in the picture, clouding her reasoning processes.

She had to get out of here, before she saw him again. Where was Chance? She had to get her dog and go home, buy herself some breathing space, find out if she really was pregnant or if she was just being hysterical.

Decide for herself—away from the hypnotic presence of her beautiful husband—if any of this was real, or if it was all part of his game. It was not as if he hadn't warned her.

That it would be complicated. That he was master of the elaborate prank.

The thought that those vows they had spoken might be part of a prank made her sick to her stomach. It was all too much. Too much had unfolded over the last month, and especially these magical days at Boy's Den.

All Krissy's old fears around family swarmed to the surface. She realized she had made a terrible mistake. She had let herself be seduced—literally and figuratively—into thinking make-believe was real. She had been pulled into a fairy tale when she of all people should have known better.

Where was Chance? The last she had seen him had been last night. He had been trailing Mike, a sleeping boy over each shoulder, to the main lodge.

The boys who had called her auntie with such excitement last night.

Her sense of loss deepened. She was not their auntie, not really. None of it was real.

She couldn't risk going to find her dog and bumping into Jonas. Besides, her dog loved it here. He loved having little boys to play with. Chance was better off without her.

Just like she was better off without Jonas.

She threw things into a bag. She paused at the white dress. She couldn't take it, this poignant reminder of the most incredible day of her life.

But she couldn't resist it, either. She stuffed the dress in her bag, scribbled a note to Jonas and went out the door. She slid through the trees like a ghost to the main gate and then the main road.

She did something she had never done before.

She stuck out her thumb. She wasn't afraid.

Jonas looked at his watch and smiled. Krissy was sleeping late. Well, who could blame her? It had been quite the night. Dawn had been breaking when they had finally collapsed into each other's arms and slept.

He grabbed her a coffee, taking great pleasure in making it exactly how she liked it, and then he made his way up to the cabin. He was going to kiss his wife awake.

He kicked open the cabin door. "Hey, Mrs. Boyden, time to—

The bed was empty. The cabin was completely empty. He thought she must have gone in search of him, but how could he have missed her? And then it occurred to him the cabin had a strange aura of abandonment clinging to it. And that her things were gone.

Even the dress that had lain in a crumpled heap by the side of the bed this morning was gone.

He felt a sense of panic rising in him. And then he saw the note, tucked under a jar that she had put her bouquet of lupines into.

Jonas raced over and picked it up, sank into a chair.

Jonas,
I am just feeling entirely overwhelmed. I feel we've been swept away by passion and realize that may not be the best way to make this kind of momentous decision. Please respect my need for some time and space.

She signed it simply *Krissy*. And then added a PS asking him to give Chance to his nephews.

His nephews. Not her nephews, as if those vows they had spoken yesterday, that joined them so completely, did not matter. As if they were not married at all.

He sank into the chair and the note trembled in his hand.

Of course she didn't trust love. She'd told him about her parents. But now he saw she didn't trust it so much that she didn't even want to risk loving her own dog.

His heart felt as if it was shattering.

For himself.

But for her, too.

And this was a truth he'd always known about love. It left you open to the worst kind of pain. A pain that felt insurmountable, as if it would never end, a gaping wound that would never heal.

Krissy was right.

They had not thought this thing through nearly enough. He was shocked at himself for allowing himself to be exactly as she had stated, *swept away by passion*.

But for him, it wasn't passion. He was no newcomer to passion. If he'd been swept away by it in the past, it had been temporary. A moment, and then he'd found his feet, himself, his equilibrium.

This was not passion that was sweeping him away.

It was love.

What did love do? Did it go after her and insist on having its own way? Did it try to convince her? Throw itself at her feet begging for mercy? Or did it respect her need for space and time, and trust that she would come to know the truth as surely as he did?

If he had to convince her that what had leaped up between them was good and real, maybe it wasn't quite as good and real as he thought it was.

Besides, who knew love's dagger more intimately than him? If he felt this bereft about losing Krissy after only knowing her for such a short time, didn't that prove what he had felt since the death of his parents? That love could cripple the strongest man?

Jonas tried to convince himself it was good that she had taken this step—declared a need for space—before it deepened even more.

He had the awful thought she might be hitchhiking. If that was the case, he had to find her for her own safety.

Besides, he realized, after the joy of last night, he could not face his family. He quickly packed his things and made his way out to the parking lot. He got in his car—the car he suddenly hated—and drove away before anyone could see him, ask painful questions, put him on the spot.

He scanned the road for Krissy. She couldn't have been gone long, and she could not have gotten far. But she was nowhere to be seen.

When it became apparent he would not find her, he finally stopped and sent his sister a quick text.

Something has come up for Krissy.

He remembered her planning an exit strategy well before all this had unfolded into such a spectacular disaster.

She's had an emergency. Can you look after the dog for now?

Then he turned off his phone before Theresa could answer. He resisted, just barely, the impulse to toss it away in a fit of fury and frustration.

CHAPTER EIGHTEEN

KRISSY LAY ON her couch. She was in her wedding dress. She had developed a terrible habit of wearing it around the house, as if she was taking some satisfaction in the fact it made her feel even worse, if that was possible.

She hadn't combed her hair yet today, and the dress had an ice cream splotch on the front of it. Prone, she trailed her hand with the spoon in it over the edge of the sofa until she hit the rim of the ice cream bucket. She dug the spoon in and lifted it to her lips.

Another splotch melted onto the dress.

She had to pull it together. Ice cream for breakfast wasn't good for the baby. The drugstore earliest alert pregnancy test kit had confirmed what her heart already knew.

A baby.

She was going to have Jonas's baby.

It made her so happy, and so sad at the same time. She would not repeat her parents' horrible story, a baby binding them together long after the passion had fizzled to ugly, wet embers.

Still, she had thought Jonas would call or drop by unexpectedly, hadn't she? Just to check on her? Just to make sure she was all right? Just because he loved her to the moon and back and couldn't stay away?

She had told him to leave her alone. He was just following instructions. She burst into tears and then tried to staunch the flow. All this emotion could not be good for the baby!

Krissy heard a vehicle pull up out front. Could he have come, after all? She got up off the sofa and flicked back the curtain. The sunlight hurt her eyes.

Not Jonas. It was a moving van. How could she have mistaken that deep rumble for the sound of his car? That was the nature of hope, perhaps, wanting something so badly it filled in the blanks with imagination. This was what her secret longing, her secret hope, had always been, even when she denied it: someone to love her. Someone to give her the family she longed for.

Two burly men were getting out of that van, sliding open the rolling door on the back of it. Good grief. Today was the day they were bringing the boxes from her aunt's office.

Had she known that? Did she have it marked on a calendar somewhere? It was summer. There was no school to keep her on schedule. No routine. The days were sliding into one another, and her responsibilities—keeping her grass cut, opening her mail, answering messages—had fallen completely by the wayside.

No one missed her.

That was how totally pathetic her life was. Why try to hide it from complete strangers? She went and opened the door. If her state of dishevelment, and her wedding dress, shocked the deliverymen, they certainly didn't show it.

She showed them where the basement door was, then ignored them as they carried boxes up and down the stairs. When had she become this person? She simply didn't care what they thought of her as she took up her reclining position on the couch.

"Ah, miss?"

"Yes?"

"We're all done. If you could sign this?"

She sat up and took the clipboard and signed.

"This fell out of one of the boxes," he said, handing her a file. "Sorry."

"It's okay." She had some money lying on

the coffee table left over from a pizza delivery, and she handed it all to him as a tip.

Then they were gone, and she stared at the two items in her hand. One was an envelope, and the other was a file that had Jonas Boyden written across the front of it in a thick black Sharpie in Aunt Jane's block printing.

Krissy realized how *hungry* she was for any smidgen of information about Jonas. How had he answered the questions on the Match Made in Heaven application? What did he do for fun? What did he consider the most important attribute in another human being?

But she forced herself to be disciplined, to calm the hammering of her heart by opening the envelope instead. Inside it was the purchase agreement for her little carriage house.

She remembered how pleased her aunt had been when she had found it and brought Krissy to see it, how excited they both had been when it was priced reasonably, well within Krissy's minuscule budget.

Now, she saw exactly why her aunt Jane's business account had been so meager. Her aunt had spent all her money when she had paid for the majority of the cost of the carriage house.

Stunned by this gift, her fingers trembling, Krissy opened the file with Jonas's name on

it. She was not sure if she was relieved or aggrieved that there was no application form
inside the thin file.

There was nothing there at all, except a
carbon copy of a receipt for five thousand
dollars with words written across it: *Satisfaction guaranteed.*

She was going to close the file when she
realized something was written on the back
of the receipt.

She turned it over.

In her aunt's spidery, oh, so familiar handwriting, were the words *Krissy's perfect
match.*

Her house. And her husband. Aunt Jane
looking after her. Except the husband part
had gone so terribly wrong.

But there was the baby. Someone to care
about. Someone to lavish love on… She heard
another vehicle stop in front of her house.
That was more traffic in the last hour than
she'd had since she arrived home from the
Boyden family reunion.

Krissy went and peeked out the curtain
again.

Finally he had come. Her relief was instant
and acute. It was real, after all. They could
figure this thing out.

But as she watched, it wasn't Jonas who

got out of the car. First it was Chance, racing toward the door, and then it was Theresa.

She might have been able to keep that door closed to Theresa, but the dog? She cried harder as she saw how fast he was running to the door. He was scratching on it, now, whining, giving hysterical little barks.

Krissy went and opened the door. She collapsed in a puddle of feeling, threw her arms around the dog, who lavished her with kisses and whined his admonishment for being abandoned.

Theresa's feet moved into her range of vision.

"Oh, my," Theresa said sadly.

And Krissy realized the sight she must make, in her crumpled, stained wedding dress, hair uncombed and eyes puffy from crying.

"Let's go in," Theresa said gently. "I'll make you a nice cup of tea." Once they were in the door, Theresa took her in solemnly, and said, "Where's your bathroom? I'm going to run you a nice bath and make you tea while you have a soak."

Stop this, Krissy ordered herself, but the truth was, she was so relieved to have someone take charge that she just pointed the way to the bathroom. While the bath

ran, she shucked the wedding dress and put
on her robe.

Minutes later, she was soaking, the dog
was hanging his head woefully over the side
of the tub, looking at her accusingly, and she
could hear Theresa humming away in her
kitchen.

It was the first time Krissy had felt sane
since she had left Boy's Den. Feeling restored
and stronger, she finally pulled herself from
the tub, wrapped herself in her robe and pad-
ded down the hall.

"How do you like our new car?" Theresa
asked her, setting a cup of tea down in front
of her and taking the seat across from her.

"He told you about the bet."

"Bet?" Theresa said, cocking her head at
Krissy. "No, he told us he hated that car. He
didn't want it anymore."

"Oh," Krissy said.

"Just for the record, he looks as bad as you.
Maybe worse."

She couldn't even be offended that Theresa
thought she looked bad. Her heart twisted at
the thought of Jonas in pain. Somehow, she
had pictured him shrugging the whole thing
off, getting back to normal quite quickly,
leaving the whole debacle behind with a certain ease.

"Maybe you'd better tell me about the bet," Theresa suggested.

"The bet. The one where Mike would get the car if Jonas turned thirty and wasn't in a committed relationship."

"That wasn't really a bet," Theresa said. "It was a joke between the three of us."

"Well, he didn't see it that way. And neither did Mike. They were laughing about it the morning after the wedding. I heard them."

"You better tell me how our silly bet relates to you," Theresa said quietly.

And suddenly Krissy needed to tell someone, as if in the telling of the entire story, she would herself be able to figure out the truth. She started at that night they had set off the alarm at Match Made in Heaven and told Theresa the entire story.

"And then today," she finally finished, nearly half an hour later, "I found this."

She went and got the receipt her aunt had written and flipped it over so Theresa could see the back of it.

Her almost sister-in-law looked at it, then sighed. "Do you think I would have pushed you two to get married if I didn't think this very same thing, Krissy? You two, together, were something to see. You know, Mike and I have the best relationship. It's as solid and as comfy as an old T-shirt you love to wear around the house.

"But you and Jonas have something else. It's the same thing I saw in my parents. It's like a light goes on in both of you when you're together, and it makes the very air around you shimmer with radiance."

"But we barely know each other!" Krissy wailed. "It started over a bet!"

"Maybe that is how it started," Theresa said, "but you can't possibly believe he married you because of that! I saw the look in his eyes. And our bets go back and forth all the time. They're games, that's all. He might have lost the car. Mike would have enjoyed tormenting him for a week or two and then made sure he won it back on a bet about a hockey game or something. So what's really going on with you?"

Krissy faced what was really going on with her. It felt like a relief to say it. "I don't want to be like my parents."

"Your parents?"

And so she ended up telling Theresa about that, too.

"And now you're going to have a baby," Theresa said.

Krissy went very still. "How do you know?"

"I'd like to tell you I can see it in you, and

I can, now that I know. But I saw the test strip in the bathroom. Did you suspect it at the reunion?"

"Yes."

"So that explains the fast exit."

"Are you going to tell him?" Krissy whispered.

"No, Krissy, I'm not. You're going to have to make that decision."

"What if I tell him, and he feels obligated to make our marriage real because of a baby?"

"Just like your parents?"

"Yes."

Theresa sighed. "This isn't about the baby, not really. It's about whether or not you love him. Because that would involve a level of trust in him. And you can't decide that based on what your aunt thought, or what I think, either. Your heart is telling you the truth, and I think you are brave enough to listen to it. But I can't make that decision for you."

As Theresa spoke, as her words washed over Krissy, it felt as if a dark curtain was being lifted and the sun was dancing back into her life.

That thing that would not be killed and would not be quelled, no matter how hard she tried. It winked back to life, an ember that had been blown on.

Hope.

A sudden illuminating realization came to her. The level of trust she needed, she realized, was not in Jonas. She needed to trust herself.

"I need to see him," Krissy said. And then she laughed. "I don't even know where my husband lives."

"Luckily for you," Theresa said, grinning, "I do."

Jonas's face itched from not shaving. His hair was too long. He could smell himself, for God's sake. His breath could make a train take a dirt road. Added to that, Jonas had the headache of all headaches. He wished he could blame it on alcohol, but no, it was heartache pure and simple. He wasn't eating right. He was barely sleeping.

How well he remembered this kind of pain from the loss of his parents.

He counted back to the day he had first met Krissy. Barely a month. If she could do this to him after one month, wasn't it for the best that she was gone? What if they'd been together a year, and she decided to pull the plug? Or two years. Or ten.

Or maybe she wouldn't make a decision to pull the plug. Maybe she would die in a terrible accident, just like his parents had.

This was what he'd forgotten when he was falling for her and falling so hard. The pain, not so much of loving, but of losing that love.

It was why he had wrestled down the desire to phone her. A thousand times he had looked up her number, thought of calling it just to hear her voice. But then, no.

He'd get through this period of grief.

He'd white-knuckle his way through it. Go cold turkey, like an addict leaving behind their drug, their source of pleasure, their *one thing* that made them want to live, that gave them the impetus to get up in the morning.

But he wasn't strong enough to go completely cold turkey. Well-meaning relatives—who had no idea his marriage was over before it had really begun—kept sending him pictures from the reunion.

The tug-of-war, her face caught in the reflected light of the fireworks, her expression as she ate her first s'more and of course, her coming toward him with those flowers in her hair and that look on her face.

That was the problem, really.

The look on her face. Nobody could make up a look like that, could they?

He groaned, back on the merry-go-round, revisiting all those things he needed to stop revisiting.

He glanced at the clock: 10:00 a.m. Today, he'd go to the office. Today, he'd make those phone calls, today he'd answer emails.

He took his phone out.

He ordered himself to look at his emails, to return a call, to look for a new resort to buy.

But instead, he opened the pictures of Krissy, felt his heart fall all over again and realized he would not be getting back to normal today.

CHAPTER NINETEEN

JONAS WOKE UP, feeling groggy and out of sorts. His teeth felt as if they were wearing socks. He glanced at the clock. It was two o'clock in the afternoon.

What kind of self-respecting person was napping at two in the afternoon?

He realized someone was at the door. You practically had to have secret service clearance to get in his building so he knew it must be Theresa.

"Go away," he called.

She knocked at the door again. He knew his sister. She wasn't going away. He got up and went to the door, flung it open.

It wasn't his sister.

Krissy stood there, with Chance.

The dog apparently had forgotten all the good things they had taught him, because he leaped at Jonas, put his paws on his shoulders and cleaned his face.

"Get off me," he bellowed.

"If I were you," Krissy said, slipping in the door completely uninvited and shutting it behind her, "I'd take kisses where you can get them. You look terrible." She wrinkled her nose. "And you smell."

He managed to get the dog off of him. "Sit down!"

The dog did so reluctantly. Jonas stared at Krissy. His wife. Unlike him, she looked at the top of her game. Not the least heartbroken, apparently. Radiant.

Beautiful in a pair of jeans and open-toed shoes and a clinging T-shirt. Her hair was flowing free around her shoulders, and he had to shove his hands in his pockets to keep from touching it.

He looked away from her so that he didn't have to see her lips. How could he look at them without remembering? Wanting? Longing?

"Sorry," Krissy said. "I had to bring Chance. He won't leave me since I left him at Boy's Den. He has anxiety now, every time I go out the door."

Perfectly understandable, Jonas thought.

"What do you want?" he asked hoarsely.

"This came in the mail," she said.

She handed him a piece of paper, and he

unfolded it, frowned at it. So much easier to study it than to look at her.

It was their certificate of marriage.

"Yeah," he said gruffly, handing her back the piece of paper without looking at her, "about that. What do you want to do? Annul it?"

"Hmm, I think you can only annul an unconsummated marriage," she said mildly.

She was going to bring *that* up? He dared a look at her. Memories of being with her in that way stormed him.

"Well, what do you want to do, then?" he managed to ask her.

"I want to give it a try," she said.

He stared at her.

"If you want to."

Want to? He wanted to throw himself at her feet and scream yes. He wanted to pick her up and swing her in circles until they were both dizzy from it.

But what if it didn't work out? What if all those scenarios he had played out in his mind over the last few days came to fruition? He would be a destroyed man.

Though, truth to tell, he was nearly a destroyed man now.

"Why?" he asked her.

Her words were so simple.

"Because I love you. Madly. Unreasonably. It feels like the air is gone from my world. The color. The reason."

But that was how he was feeling.

"I know you're scared, Jonas."

He wanted to deny he was scared, but when he looked at her, she was the one who would always know all of him.

And who would accept it. Maybe even cherish that which he tried to hide from the rest of the world.

"I am, too," she said. "Terrified. Both of us have been so wounded by love. In very different ways, but it still makes it hard to say yes to it. I think that's why I was so quick to reach the wrong conclusion when I overheard you talking to Mike on Sunday morning."

"What?"

"He was congratulating you on the lengths you'd gone to to get your car back."

"It stopped being about the car a long, long time ago."

"I know that," she said softly. "I needed it to be about the car. Because I had to run. I was so afraid, Jonas."

"Of me?" he asked, appalled.

"No, Jonas. Of repeating history. I'm going to have a baby. Our baby."

He could feel something rising within him, phoenixlike, out of the ashes of his destruction.

He stepped toward her, and then closer.

"A baby?" he said. "Our baby?"

She nodded, and it was all there. Her terror. Her uncertainty.

He put his hands on her shoulders and rested his forehead against hers. The moment he touched her, his strength began to flow back into him. She was Samson's hair and Arthur's sword.

"I was born for this," he told her softly.

"To be a daddy?" she asked.

"Maybe that, too, but no. I was born to take that fear from you, and that uncertainty. I was born to show you a world that can be trusted. I was born to show you what love can do, and what it can make and how incredible the world can be because of it."

She was crying now. He wrapped his arms around her and held her tight.

"Jonas?"

"Yes, my love?"

"You really stink."

And just like that, they were laughing. And the dog was barking, and the world and the future stretched out in front of them, illuminated.

Illuminated by the one light that had illuminated the world forever. Sometimes it flickered, sometimes it was hard to see. Sometimes tumult and the unexpected and uncertainty threatened it.

And yet it always fluttered back to life, it always gained strength, it always proved itself more powerful than any darkness.

There it was, shining.

A beacon for all to follow.

Love.

EPILOGUE

"ARE YOU SURE?" Jonas asked Krissy.

"About?"

"Leaving her with the boys."

"Jonas! We are not leaving Jane with the boys. We're leaving her with your sister. I think she can be trusted with a baby."

Jane-Paulette was named after Krissy's aunt Jane, of course, and after Jonas's mother. She was nearly four months old.

And so tiny. And so perfect. Jonas had never felt anything like what he felt the first time he had held that baby. Protective. Besotted. Enchanted. And you would think that feeling would go away—the newness would rub off the awe—but no, it deepened.

"You told me you were going to take away my fear and uncertainty," Krissy reminded him. "You told me you were going to teach me the world can be trusted."

"And haven't I?" he demanded.

"Oh, yeah, you have. But honestly, Jonas, when it comes to the baby, I have to teach you all those things."

"She's little! Simon and Gar are rambunctious. You can't be too careful."

"You can, actually, be too careful. If she's survived Chance, the probability of her surviving our nephews is pretty good."

The reunion was starting tomorrow. But Jonas and Krissy and Jane and the dog had all arrived early. Because Krissy had announced to him, her eyes shining, that she finally had figured out where to spread her aunt's ashes.

When she had told him, he'd had his doubts.

"But you said she wanted them spread in the place she loved most. She's never even been to Boy's Den."

Krissy smiled at him tenderly, that smile that could still melt his heart, even as they approached their one-year anniversary.

"What she loved most was love," she told him. "That's where she would want to be."

So Jonas reluctantly surrendered the baby to his sister and followed Krissy down to the rowboat. She had the urn of ashes on her lap.

"Where to?" he asked, gathering up the oars.

"You know," she said.

And then he did.

They had honeymooned here, last year, after all the vacationers had gone home. And they had taken out the rowboat and found the most beautiful private cove overlooking the lake. It had its own beach and was only visible from the water.

And it had a For Sale sign on it.

They had wandered that piece of property most of the day, deciding where to put the road and where their cabin would go, where they would put the tire swing over the water, where a good place for a sandbox would be.

Now he turned the boat in that direction and rowed through quiet waters.

They came to the cove. Their new house was rising out of the ground, the framing nearly done.

Already, Jonas could feel the long summer days that would unfold here. He could hear children laughing and dogs barking. He could smell campfires burning and marshmallows cooking. He could see Krissy reading on the deck and a little girl with blueberry stains around her mouth. He could see himself and another child carrying a string of fish up from the dock. For one brief, incredible moment, he could see the future.

"Are you ready?" he asked softly.

With reverent fingers, she unscrewed the lid from the urn. She held the open mouth over the water and the ashes spilled out in a silver trail across it.

He thought of that strange woman whom he had only met once, how he had felt she had seen his soul and known things about him no one could know.

He thought of how she had loved Krissy, how she had kept that little spark of belief in love alive in Krissy, when her childhood experiences could have snuffed it out for good.

He knew he owed this woman in some way. Jonas was well aware he did not know how these things worked, but that did not stop him from being grateful, daily, that it had worked. That Aunt Jane had, from heaven, made them, Jonas and Krissy, her most perfect match.

"Thank you," he said softly, and Krissy smiled.

It was that smile that lit his world, and that he saw on his child's perfect little lips. It was a smile that let him know, over and over again, that the world was full of distractions. Wealth and success, toys and games like the ones he used to play.

But in the end, all that mattered was what that smile told him.

Jonas knew Krissy had been absolutely right about putting these ashes in this tiny lake where her aunt had never visited.

Aunt Jane would want to be right here. In her favorite place.

Where the love was.

* * * * *

*If you enjoyed this story,
check out these other great reads from
Cara Colter*

One Night with Her Brooding Bodyguard
Cinderella's New York Fling
Tempted by the Single Dad
Cinderella's Prince Under the Mistletoe

All available now!